I0640806

Edward Walford

Louis Napoleon - the former emperor of the french

A biography

Edward Walford

Louis Napoleon - the former emperor of the french
A biography

ISBN/EAN: 9783742867186

Manufactured in Europe, USA, Canada, Australia, Japa

Cover: Foto ©Raphael Reischuk / pixelio.de

Manufactured and distributed by brebook publishing software
(www.brebook.com)

Edward Walford

Louis Napoleon - the former emperor of the french

PREFACE.

— —

HAVING been called upon, almost at an hour's notice, to put together a short biography of the late Emperor, I can pretend to little or nothing of originality, beyond some few anecdotes towards the end of the work, which have come to me on the authority of a member of the family of the late Sir John Bowring.

For the most part these pages are a "cento," made up from sketches of the Emperor's career published in the *Morni11gPost,* the *Standard,* and in a number of Messrs. Chambers's Tracts, which I wrote in 1869, just before the outbreak of the Franco-German war.

Whilst weaving these, as I hope, into a connected story, I have found it impossible in every case to specify my authority for each paragraph ; and I can only hope that the public will view with indulgence a memoir compiled-I will not say written-within four brief days.

HAMPSTEAD, N. W.,
lall. 13, 1873.

CONTENTS.

— —

LOUIS NAPOLEON,

EX~EMPEROR OF THE FRENCH.

CHAPTER I.

THE BONAPARTE FAMILY.

IT has been repeatedly asserted in various works of greater or less authority, that the family of Bonaparte, or Buonaparte, from which the &x· Imperial house of France is sprung, came originally from Tuscany; it is an acknowledged fact also, that they had been settled in the Island of Corsica for many generations before the birth of the first Emperor Napoleon, an event which happened, as every Englishman knows, at Ajaccio, in that island, on the 15th of August, 1769. It is certain, how· ever, that as early as the fourteenth or fifteenth century, Bonapartes belonged to the Island of Majorca ; and it is more than probable that these, as well as those of Corsica, were branches of one and the same noble family. It is certain also, that there is extant, a comedy written by one Nicolo Buonaparte, of San Miniato, a citizen of Florence, entitled "La Vedova," which was published at Florence in 1568; and a narrative* of the pillage of Rome under Charles V., which appeared at Cologne in 1736, bears on its title page the name.of one Jacopo Buonaparte. On the other hand, Colonel J. Mitchell, the author of the" Fall of Napoleon,"] informs us that the information which he gathered in the course of certain researches made some thirty years since, in the Balearic Isles, regarding the Bonaparte family, was such as to induce him to believe that they were originally of French extraction, and had emigrated thither from Provence, probably by way of Genoa. If this really be the case, it is strange that the Spanish origin of the family-for a residence of some centuries in the Balearic Isles amounts to that-was apparently unknown to the public, or even to antiquaries, during the reign of the first Emperor Napoleon, and that it was never claimed or pleaded by Joseph Bonaparte as a title to the support or allegiance of his Spanish subjects and fellow countrymen during the time that he sat on the throne of that country, between the years 1808 and 1813.

On the other hand, however, there is the formal testimony of Don Antonio Furio, Member of the Royal Academy of Literature of Barcelona, and

* "Ragguaglio Storico del Sacco di Roma dell' anno 1527." Cologne. 1736.

t "The Fall of Napoleon; an Historical Memoir; "by Lieut.-Col. J. Mitchell, H.P., author of the "Life of Wallenstein," &c. 3 vols: London. G. W. Nickisson, Regent-street. 1846.

"Chronologer-General" of the Island of Majorca, who certifies that "an examination of the books and documents which he had inspected, bears evidence of the origin, rank, dignity, and extinction of the noble family of Bonaparte in this Island of Majorca. For, in a book preserved in the archives of the City of Palma, in which are contained the armorial bearings of the noble families of the island, appear those of Bonaparte, which are emblazoned in the following manner :-Dexter, *azure,* with six stars in pairs *or;* sinister, *gules,* with a lion rampant *or.* The chief *or,* with an Eagle saliant, *sable.*

"The book already named," he adds, " bears farther evidence to show that the family of Bona· parte came from Genoa to Majorca, and was always looked upon as belonging to the equestrian order, and that its members held rank and filled various honourable offices suited to their dignity.

"It is not many years ago since the armorial bearings above described were to be seen on a monument in the convent of the nuns of St. Augustin in this city, as well as on one in front of the church of the monastery of St. Geronimo. The same arms are also engraved on the family sepulchre in the cloister of the convent belonging to the order of St. Domingo, and mentioned in the following words in the original register of interments of that convent, formed in the seventeenth century :-' In the Chapel of Our Lady of Grace and o(St. Blaise the Martyr, is the ancient tomb of the Bonapartes, as proved by the armorial-bearings of the family in the said chapel.'

" From another and more ancient book of interments formed in 1559, and kept in the archives of the above-named convent, the antiquity and nobility of the Bonapartes is also proved. At page g6, and under the title of 'Graves of Persons of Rank,' it is said, 'The Bonapartes have their tomb marked with their shield and armorial-bearings, in the cloister and chapel of Our Lady.'

"Our historians farther attest the nobility of the Bonaparte family, and speak of its distinguished members, among whom is particularly mentioned the learned jurist, Don Hugo Bonaparte, who left this island in 1411, and settled in Corsica, where he became President of the Council. How he came to be inscribed on the Golden Book of France, does not appear.

"The departure of this individual did not, however, occasion the extinction of the Bonapartes in Majorca : for in the History of the island, written by Don Vincente Mut, and printed at Palma in 1650, it is stated (Book V. page 269,) that when the commons rose against the tyrants who governed for the Emperor Charles V., the nobles took part with the sovereign ; but finding themselves too weak to contend against their more numerous adversaries, they resolved to apply to the king for a remedy: and one of the subscribers to this petition, made in 1521, was Baptista Bonaparte. It is not known whether the family became extinct during the wars of the commons ; but in the last chapter of his work, Don Vincente Mut states, that it no longer existed in 1650. 'There -have died out,' he says, ' or become extinct, eighty-four equestrian names, though descendants of these houses still exist in other families ;' " and among these he enumerates the Bonapartes. "The work of Don Vincente has always been looked upon as containing an accurate register of the noble houses that have become extinct; and history and our public monuments furnish no further information on the subject."

It should be added, however, that other coats of arms, also ascribed to families of the name of Buonaparte, have been discovered in various parts of the south ; though none of the statements which claim for the Corsican family an ancient and noble Italian descent, rest on documents of equal authenticity with those of the Balearic Islands.

Be their origin, however, as it may, one thing is certain, namely, that the Bonapartes of Ajaccio, though they had fallen into comparative poverty, were reckoned as nobles and not as plebeians, a little more than a century ago, when the first Emperor came into the world. He was the second son of Carlo Bonaparte and his wife, Letizia Ramolini, both natives of Corsica; the house in which he was born still stands, forming one side of a court leading out of the Rue Charles; and recent travellers tell us that the room is still shown in which he first saw the light. Charles Bonaparte, *pere,* had been bred up for the profession of the law, and, curiously enough, before the birth of his distinguished son, he had served under Paoli, in defence of his country against the French, to whom the Genoese had basely sold the island. The submission of Corsica to France, however, had been completed in June, 1769, a month or two before the birth of the first Emperor, who consequently was born a French citizen. In the following September, when Count Marbceuf, the French Commissioner, convoked by the King's Letters Patent the States of Corsica, consisting of three orders-nobility, clergy, and commons-the family of Bonaparte, having shown their titles, was registered among the nobility ; and some years later, Charles Bonaparte himself was sent as a member of a deputation of his order to Louis XVI. He was soon afterwards appointed Assessor to the Judicial Court of Ajaccio, a post which he was the more glad to undertake, owing to his straitened circumstances and the prospect of a young family, for he had spent most of his little property in a bad speculation in some salt manufactories, after having previously lost a law-suit which he had instituted for his inheritance.

CHAPTER II.

LOUIS NAPOLEON'S PARENTS.

No doubt the feeling that his father was poor, though his family was noble, acted in the breast of Napoleon I. as a strong incentive to action, and proved the first step in that career which culminated in the Imperial dignity which he eventually attained, and from which he was only cast down by the firm and steady resistance of England to his ambitious designs. By his first wife, the cruelly-wronged Empress Josephine, the Emperor had no issue ; and though his second spouse, Maria Louisa, brought him, in 1811, a son, the "King of Rome," yet the latter scarcely survived his boyhood, dying, unmarried, in July, 1832. Having gained the Imperial throne for himself, however, it was but natural that, long before the birth of his only son, he should have desired to secure the succession for his family; and accordingly, by certain Imperial Edicts, issued in 1804 and 1805, the Emperor formally set aside the usual order of descent by primogeniture, and declared that the succession to the Imperial Crown should be vested in the family of the fourth of his brothers, Louis, whom he created King of Holland, and who afterwards became the father of the subject of the present biographical sketch. In order to understand the position which the future restorer of the Imperial name to France occupied in his childhood, it may be desirable to give a brief outline of his father's life; and this I do in the words of a writer in the " English Cyclopcedia"* :-

" Louis Napoleon Bonaparte, the fourth son of Charles Bonaparte, and father of Napoleon Ill., was born at Ajaccio, in Corsica, on the arst of September, 1778. At an early age he entered the French army, and accompanied his brother Napoleon to Italy and Egypt. In Italy he distinguished himself at the passage of the bridge of Arcola, braving the fire of the enemy, and shielding the body of his brother and commander. When Napoleon became first consul he was sent on a mission to St. Petersburg ; but on arriving at Berlin he learned the news of the death of the Emperor Paul. He returned to Paris after remaining at Berlin about a year, and became a general of brigade, a counsellor of state, and afterwards a general of division. In 1802 he married Hortense Eugenie de Beauharnais, the daughter of the Empress Josephine. When Napoleon became Emperor, Louis was promoted to higher honours, and was made

* "English Cyclopeedia of Biography," by Charles Knight: London, Bradbury & Evans, 1856.

Governor of Piedmont, and afterwards commanded the army of the north of Holland. After the Batavian Republic had been converted into a kingdom, the States of Holland, in June, 1806, sent an embassy to Napoleon, requesting that Louis might be their king, which was granted, and he immediately assumed the title. He strenuously exerted himself to better the condition of his people, and distinguished himself on several occasions by his personal humanity. His love for his people occasioned him to refuse without hesitation the offer made him by his brother of the crown of Spain ; but his opposition to Napoleon's plans, which he thought were prejudicial to their welfare, gave great satisfaction at Paris. His wife was a most attached adherent of Napoleon, and her inability to control her husband, the death of her eldest son, in 1807, and the state of her health, induced her to repair to Paris, where a third son was born. She was afterwards sent by Napoleon, in 1809, to induce Louis to comply with his wishes, but Louis refused. She then returned to Paris, where she resided in state as Queen of Holland; and Napoleon sent Oudinot, with 20,000 men, against Louis, who thereupon abdicated in favour of his son, which abdication Napoleon rejected ; and on the 9th of July, 1810, Holland was united to the Empire. Louis retired to Gratz, in Styria, where he lived three years under the title of Due de St. Leu, and his wife became wholly separated from him, though not divorced. In 1813, when the allies appeared about to fall upon France, Louis offered his services to the Emperor, by whom they were accepted ; and he proceeded to Switzerland, but he was not employed.   On the downfall of Napoleon, when the Dutch threw off the French yoke, Louis addressed a letter to the provisional government from Soleure, asserting his claims to the throne, but they were rejected.   He then commenced a suit at Paris for the restitution of his two sons, then living under the care of their mother, who had obtained a grant of the domain of St. Leu, with the title of Duchess, through the interest of the Emperor Alexander.   The return of Napoleon put a stop to the suit, and the Duchess of St. Leu did the honours of Napoleon's Court, and used her interest in favour of the unfortunate of all parties.   After the battle of Waterloo she went to reside in Switzerland, with her sons ; whilst Louis retired to the Papal States, where others of his family had assembled, and devoted himself chiefly to literature.   He published ' Marie, ou Les Hollandaises,' ' Documens Historiques sur la Hollande ' (five volumes, octavo), which appeared in 1820 ; ' Memoires sur la Versification ;' an opera, a tragedy, a collection of poems, and a reply to Sir Walter Scott on his 'History of Napoleon.'   He died at Leghorn on the 15th of June, 1846 ; and at his special desire, which after some delay was acceded to, his body was buried at St. Leu, in France, with those of his father and his first son, on the 29th of September, 1847."

Hortense, whom I have already named as the mother of the future Emperor, was a lady of too marked individuality of character, and exerted too decided an influence on her son's life and career, to be passed by without a few words descriptive of her. She was the beautiful, amiable, and accomplished daughter of the Empress Josephine, by her first husband, the Viscount de Beauhamais. The marriage was not altogether a happy one; but young, handsome, graceful, and courteous in manner, and also a musician and a poetess, Hortense speedily became known to the French people as the composer of the song and march, " Partant pour la Syrie," at the stirring tones of which the heart of many a Frenchman has been made to beat alike in the French camp and at the French Court. She was also, as I have said, a favourite with the Emperor himself, who knew that her marriage with his brother had been not the result of affection but an act of obedience to his will-a sacrifice made in order to support and secure his throne, and who therefore showered honours thickly down upon her husband, making him successively *Grand Connltable* of France, Governor of Piedmont, and ultimately King of Holland. This kingdom, it may here be remarked by way of parenthesis, Louis resigned, not long after the birth of the future Emperor of the French, in consequence of an honourable and high-minded conviction that he could not hold it consistently with the interests of Holland, and at the same time with the ties which bound him to his

brother and to France.   The marriage of Hortense
de Beauharnais with Louis Bonaparte was blessed
by the Church in the person of the Cardinal Caprera ;
for the stepfather of the bride, as First Consul, had
already become convinced of the expediency of
ecclesiastical re-establishment in France.

Queen Hortense died, at the Swiss Castle of
Arenenberg, in October, 1837, amid the regrets of all
who had known her, when, in the flower of her life,
she graced the Courts of the Hague and the
Tuileries, and lamented by her friends and neigh-
bours in the land of her adoption.

CHAPTER III.

LOUIS NAPOLEON: HIS BIRTH AND CHILDHOOD.

THE distinguished person an outline of whose life I have undertaken to compile rather than to write, was one who, for the last half century-in fact, since the death of his uncle, the first founder of the Imperial dynasty of France-has occupied a foremost place in the history, not only of his own country, but also of Europe; and although he has died discrowned and in exile, yet it was given to him for many years, more exclusively than to any one individual of our time, to hold in his hands the destinies of Europe .. We live too near to the latter portion of his career, at all events, to be able to take an impartial view of many events in which he took the leading part, or rightly to appreciate his actions in their motives and their consequences. I shall therefore content myself with presenting my readers with a brief outline of the leading facts of his life, leaving it for other writers to enlarge upon them in the way of comment when the hand of time has revealed them in their true proportions.

Louis Napoleon-or, to give him his full baptismal name, Charles Louis Napoleon-Bonaparte was the youngest and last surviving son of Louis Bonaparte, sometime King of Holland, who was himself a younger brother of the great Napoleon. He was literally born " in the purple," for his birth took place at the Palace of the Tuileries-or, according to another account, in what is now the Rue Lafitte-on .the aoth of April, 1808 ; and the roar of cannon by which his birth was announced to the citizens of Paris was all the more loud and joyous because it conveyed to them an increased assurance of the permanence of the Imperial throne ; for was not that little infant a second heir presumptive to the honours of the as yet childless Emperor? He was baptised at the old historic palace of Fontainebleau, on the roth day of November, 18 Io, by the names of Charles Louis Napoleon. Napoleon I. stood godfather to the infant prince, and Marie Louise, the then new Empress, as his godmother, presented him at the font ; the ceremony was performed by Cardinal Fesch. The first of his three names seems soon by common family consent to have been dropped, and it was therefore by the two latter names, now familiar to the whole world, that the prince, who was destined to play so remarkable and illustrious a part in the world, was known in childhood.

Of the two elder brothers of the subject of this memoir, the first born, though baptised by the Pope-who came for that purpose all the way from Rome to St. Cloud - died in infancy from an attack of measles ; and· the next in age was carried off by an attack of fever at Forli, in Italy, in the month of March, 1831. Thus it will be seen that during his infancy and childhood there were two lives between him and the line of Imperial succession-that of the Duke of Reichstadt, or, as he was called in early life, the "King of Rome," and that also of his own elder brother. Yet it would seem that, whatever the reason may have been, even from his infancy the young Louis Napoleon was the greatest of favourites with his uncle the Emperor, who took especial pleasure in associating him with himself, and in making him bear a part in the military pageantry which represented to the dazzled eyes of Franee the glory which his right hand had achieved for her; his name, too, we are told, was written by his uncle's order, at the head of the family register of the Napoleon dynasty. Nor, in spite of the Emperor's second marriage with Marie Louise, was the young son of Hortense excluded from the society of his grandmother, the ex-Empress, who, though divorced from selfish considerations, and sacrificed as a wife to political exigencies, still resided at the Chateau of Malmaison, not far from Paris, seeking=-and finding, too-in the society of Hortense and her children the only consolation possible. under the cruel circumstances which surrounded her. Even at that early period of his life, however, the youthful Louis Napoleon must have formed a link of common interest between the Emperor and his discrowned wife. And apparently his affections were to a great extent divided between them ; for, whilst his whole subsequent life was consecrated to his uncle's memory in his thoughts, words, and deeds, it was in the name of his grandmother Josephine-as will be seen presently-that he formally announced to the Senate of France his own intended marriage with the Empress Eugenie.

The first seven years of the prince's life were spent for the most part at the Tuileries and at St. Leu, under the care of his excellent and accomplished mother, who herself taught him the first elements of the various branches of knowledge. He was a clever child, and from the first was remarkable for his love of knowledge ; and his powers of observation and reflection were drawn out and developed sensibly and prudently under her own eye. But before her little son had completed his eighth year, the throne of Napoleon had fallen, apparently never to rise again. The Emperor himself was not only in exile, but a prisoner on the barren rock of St. Helena; the Bourbons, in the person of Louis XVIII., had once more been placed, by the aid of England and her allies, upon the throne on which they had sat for nearly a thousand years; and the family of Bonaparte, young and old, root and branch, had been pro· scribed and exiled by Jaw, and forbidden to set foot upon the soil of that France which their head and chief had done so much to raise in the scale of nations.

It was in the year 1814 that the Empress Jose·

phine died at Malmaison-it is said, of a broken
heart ; for although no longer by his side as his
wife, Josephine loved the Emperor too well to sur-
vive his abdication and exile to the Island of Elba.
Her son, Eugene de Beauharnais, had been made
Viceroy of Italy; and the restoration of the
Bourbons to the throne of France was the occasion
of his recall to Paris, where every honour due to a
noble enemy was paid to him, as well as to his
sister Hortense and her sons. It was at this time
that the child Louis Napoleon was saluted by the
Emperor Alexander of Russia and the King of
Prussia in terms significant of his illustrious position, when the following episode occurred. I give
it as told in a biography of his Majesty, published
in a tract by Messrs. Chambers of Edinburgh :-

" The boy looked from the Russian Emperor to the
Prussian King, who stood near him, and then turning to
Mademoiselle de Cochelet, his governess, he asked : ' Mademoiselle, are these two gentlemen my uncles also? How
must we call them?' She told him that they, unlike the
monarchs he had been accustomed to see, were not his
uncles ; but that, nevertheless, he must address them as
' Sire.' ' But are they the enemies of my uncle ? ' asked the
boy. ' If so, why did the Emperor of Russia embrace me ? '
Mademoiselle de Cochelet explained to the young prince
that the Emperor of Russia was a private friend although a
political enemy ; and with such success did she make her
charge understand this lesson, never afterwards to be forgotten by him, that upon the next occasion when Alexander
reappeared at Malmaison the boy voluntarily presented his
Imperial Majesty with the thing which at that time he most
valued, namely, a ring which his uncle Eugene de Beau-

harnais had given to him. This ring the Emperor of Russia fastened to his watch-chain, and cherished for the sake of its young donor as long as he lived."

In 1815, upon Napoleon's escape from Elba, and reappearance before the dazzled eyes of his subjects for the" Hundred Days," Queen Hortense did the honours of the Palace of the Tuileries. She with her two sons were with the. Emperor when, on the eve of his departure for Waterloo, he distributed the Imperial eagles of France to his troops on the Champ de Mars. The young Louis Napoleon beheld and participated in that celebrated scene, and was close to his illustrious kinsman when, with drums beating, bells ringing, and martial music resounding, all France seemed to echo with the shouts of "Vive l'Empereur ! " They were all three with him also when, defeated at Waterloo, he returned for a brief moment to France, and then prepared to leave her for his last exile ; they were with him, *too,* at the last moment when he bade farewell for ever to that country which by him had for a time been made almost omnipotent. Louis Napoleon was with his illustrious uncle at Malmaison, when he started on the fatal journey which resulted in his captivity at St. Helena. lie was then about seven years of age, and the story is told how that on this occasion the young Louis Napoleon climbed on the Emperor's knee, and entreated him to remain at home ; for that if he went, his enemies would take him away and that he should never see him again. The Emperor was much affected by the child's speech,

and handed him back to his mother, saying:
"Take your son, Hortense, and look well to him;
perhaps, after all, he is the hope of my race."

Like the rest of the Bonapartes, the ex-King of
Holland and his Queen, Hortense, reduced as it
were to a private station, found themselves obliged,
at the end of the war in 1815, to withdraw from
France. The latter successively retired to Geneva;
to Aix, in Savoy, where she had founded an hospital; to Baden, in Bavaria, in order to be near her
son Eugene; and lastly to Switzerland and Rome.
She resided for some eight years at the Augsburg
Gymnasium, which she at last left in order to take
up her abode on the banks of Lake Constance, in
the canton of Thurgovia. In her maternal solici-
tude, Queen Hortense did her utmost to make of
her two sons men and citi,ens worthy of both
their country and their name, omitting neither the
culture of the mind and heart, nor the training and
exercising of the body.

Louis Napoleon received his early education in
the Castle of Arenenberg, on the shores of Lake
Constance, where he passed six years under the
supervision of his mother, from the Abbe Bertrand and M. Philippe Le Bas, and it is said
that he proved anything but a slothful pupil;
he was afterwards placed in the grammar school
at Augsburg, where he displayed quite a passion for history and the exact sciences. His
fondness for athletic exercises was equally con-
spicuous; he was one of the best fencers, riders,

and swimmers in the whole school. In Switzerland his inclination and aptitude for military strategy, especially in artillery and engineering, was first developed. He studied military science at Thun, under the direction of General Dufour, and he even served for some time as a volunteer in the Federal camp at that place, and at a later period in his life wrote a " Manuel d'Artillerie " (published at zurich in 1836), based to a great extent on his experimental training at this time, and published for the use of the officers of that arm of the service in the Helvetian Republic. As a boy he became a proficient in mathematics and fortification, and especially in the science of government, of political and military organisation ; he read much, and thought more, upon all subjects connected with the material and social happiness of nations ; he studied history, both ancient and modern, and with a watchful eye as to the true application of its lessons and warnings; and, on reaching manhood, though perhaps deficient in that practical experience which is learned in the busy world alone, he was probably better versed in the politics of Europe than many a grey-haired statesman.

But at Arenenberg he learned even more than this. To use the words of Messrs. Chambers's Tract already quoted above," It was the aim and study of Hortense to train up her son so as to serve his country either as its sovereign-if such should be the will of Providence-or as a simple soldier in the ranks ; and so it was that her son took advantage of the military camp at Thun to make himself practically acquainted with the duties of a private soldier. Every year he carried the knapsack on his back, ate the soldier's fare, handled the shovel, the pick-axe, and the wheelbarrow; learned to scale the heights of the mountains, and followed the marches of the soldiers, and returned at night to repose under a soldier's tent. Such were the lessons of self-command, of willing submission to hardship and discipline, which the prince, at his mother's wish, imposed on himself, in pursuit of that practical experience which, in every path of life, is the secret of success, and without which even the highest scientific attainments are so often valueless. It is well that those who aspire to command should first learn to obey ; that those who look forward to administering the discipline of an army or a nation, should first submit to discipline in their own persons. Had the Bourbons known, qr been taught to follow such a course, it is possible that the French Revolution, the Consulate, and the Empire, would never have arisen, and that the line of Capet would still have been seated, in power and honour, in the court of the Tuileries."

CHAPTER IV.

LOUIS NAPOLEON   HIS EARLY MANHOOD.

IN the singular career of the late Emperor, as in that of most remarkable men, there are breaks which divide it into distinct periods, without injuring the general dramatic unity. He was born seemingly to greatness. Apparently it threatened to elude him. He struggled after it in the face of adverse circumstances from the time he attained to years of discretion. He partly achieved it, partly had it thrust upon him, and after a success which should have satisfied his wildest dreams, he ended his active life, an exile as he had begun it. His youth, as will be seen, was for the most part spent far from the country of which he was by birth a citizen, and over which one day he was destined to rule as Emperor.

Next to the pale reminiscences of Court page· antries in his early childhood, nothing, perhaps, so powerfully contributed to form the character of the future Emperor as the influence of the mother in whose house he grew up as an only child. The marriage of Hortense with Louis Bonaparte was, by his confession,"forced and ill-assorted." Seven months before the birth of their third son the Royal couple parted never to be re-united. It was not without contention that the ex-King of Holland, who now called himself the Due de Saint *Leu,* made good his claims to his elder *son,* leaving the younger in the undisputed possession of the mother. Charmed as she seemed with her retirement at Arenenberg, Hortense, however, not unfrequently spent the winter in Italy, chiefly at Rome. Under the ascendency of such a mother, it was impossible that the aspiring youth could learn resignation to a humble lot. Louis Napoleon was taught to look for a change with as full a confidence as he would expect daylight at the close of the natural period of darkness. It little mattered when, where, or by what means the turn in his fortunes might come. Enough that an opening would be made. ' The Man ' was there,-and he would not have to wait long for' the Hour.'

The opportunity arrived, perhaps sooner than was expected by ' the Man,' who, however, was in readiness to seize on any chance that might offer itself. The echo of the Revolution of July, 1830, which struck his ear amid the Swiss mountains, inspired him with joy and hope. He expected that the law which banished his family from France would be repealed, and accordingly, as soon as Louis Philippe was chosen King, the Bonaparte Princes asked permission to return. The application having been refused, both Louis Napoleon and his elder brother went to Italy, and took a leading part in the rising in the Papal States. They were marching on Rome at the head of the rebels who were besieging Civita-Castellana when they were recalled by the Revolutionary Committee to Forli, where the elder brother, after an illness of two days, died at the age of twenty-one years. Louis, who fled to Ancona, was also seized with a dangerous attack of illness, from which he recovered very much in consequence of the care of his mother. At the close of 1831 General Cniarewicz and Count Plater offered Prince Louis Napoleon the command . of the insurrectionary Polish army, but he had only commenced his departure when the news arrived of the capture of Warsaw. Once more he turned his eyes towards France, and asked permission to live there, not as a Prince, but as a citizen. The only reply of the French Government was a renewal of the decree of banishment against the members of the Bonaparte family. The death of the Duke of Reichstadt, the first Emperor's only son, on the aand of July, 1832, made Louis Napoleon the next heir in the order of Imperial succession; but, though his ambition might have been stimulated by the event, there seemed at this. epoch little prospect of his ever wearing the Imperial mantle. He therefore turned his attention to study and literature, and, if his publications were not marked by any extraordinary talent, at all events they served to keep his name before the public. His" Political Reveries," "A Project of a Constitution," " Political and Military Considerations on Switzerland," and the "Manual of Artillery," already referred to, were published between 1832 and 1836. The Republican party in France naturally regarded him with sympathy, on the double ground that his writings were strongly tinged with Democratic ideas, and that Louis Philippe's Government was departing more and more from the principles to which it owed its existence. When Armand Carrel wrote in the *N'ational* "that the works of Louis Napoleon Bonaparte evinced a strong mind and a noble character," that able Republican writer little suspected that " the strong mind and the noble character" would one day be found to destroy the Republic itself.

About this time it was suggested that Louis ·Napoleonwould be a most suitable husband for the young Queen of Portugal, Donna Maria, who had lately been left a widow. Many were the competitors for her hand ;· but few, perhaps, were thought more eligible partners than a Prince who, whilst free of all engagements which could create any political complications, was closely related to an Imperial House and heir to its honours. The Queen herself, it was confidently stated at the time, was not averse to the proposal ; but Louis Napoleon declined the proffered honour, apparently for more motives than one. The chief reason, perhaps, why he refused to share a foreign throne being the visionary claims which he had at that time to the throne of France, as he indeed set forth in writing to the Queen of Portugal:-

" The noble conduct of my father, who abdicated a throne in 1810, because he could not unite the interests of France with those of Holland, has not left my memory. My father, by his example, proved to me how far the claims of one's native land are to be preferred even to a throne in a foreign country. I feel, in fact, that, trained as I have been from. infancy to cherish the thought of my own country above every other consideration, I should not be able to hold any-thing in higher esteem than the interests of France. Per-suaded as I am that the great name which I bear, and which must ever recall the memory of 15 years of glory, will not always be proscribed by my countrymen, I wait with patience in a free and hospitable land the arrival of the day when the French nation will call back to its bosom those who, in 1815, were driven into exile by the will of 200,000 strangers. This hope of being able to serve France even yet as a citizen and a soldier is that which gives strength to my soul, and, in my opinion, is worth all the thrones in the world."

While the most fulsome laudations were being bestowed on Louis Philippe, the "Citizen King," and his government, it was quite clear to those who could read the signs of the times aright that his throne was anything but secure, and that the reactionary policy of the King and his Ministers was precipitating the Orleans dynasty to its fall. Louis Napoleon rejoiced over the mistakes of the " Napoleon of Peace," and he watched his oppor-tunity. Having no faith in the stability of the throne of Louis Philippe, believing in the dis-affection of the bourgeoisie, relying on the strength of his name and the memories of the Imperial glories, Louis Napoleon resolved to escape from the obscurity of his exile, and to risk his life for a crown. He engaged in the Strasburg expedition with ardour and confidence, but with a miscalculation of the means of success, which covered the attempt and its author with ridicule. At the baths of Baden he entered into treasonable correspondence with several of the officersof the Strasburg garrison,and particularly with ColonelVaudrey, the Commander of the 4th Regiment of Artillery, in which the future Emperor made his first essay in arms, and in which the traditions and ideas of the Empire prevailed extensively. Overtures were made to Lieutenant-General Voirol, commanding the Department of the Lower Rhine, who not only rejected them, but communicated their tenor to the Prefect of the Department and to the War Office. In a clandestine visit which he made to Strasburg a plan of operations was agreed upon by the Prince and Colonel Vaudrey. He believed strongly that after once getting a footing among the troops both the army and the people would pronounce in his favour. Proclamations were prepared, which were to be distributed during his triumphal march from Strasburg to Paris; and a Democratic *rlgime* was to be inaugurated under a Napoleonic chief.

On October 25th he took leave of his mother, under the pretence that he was going to hunt ; and arrived in Strasburg on the 28th, at ten in the evening. He found Colonel Vaudrey, who had had time to reflect on the obstacles and difficultiesof

D

the enterprise, dejected and hopeless; but the resolution of the Prince was inflexible; he was, moreover, encouraged by the enthusiasm of Lieutenant
Parquin, and the decision of M. de Persigny; and
at a meeting which took place next day, the plan of
operations, in all its details, was agreed to.

At five o'clock on the morning of the 30th,
Colonel Vaudrey assembled his troops in his tents,
and presented them to the Prince, who addressed
them, and said that between him and them there
existed grand recollections. They proceeded to
the quarters of the general, who, because he would
not join in the conspiracy, was made prisoner in his
own house. The battalion of Pontoniers had been
gained over by Lieutenant Laity ; the telegraph
station was seized, and proclamations to the army
and nation were printed in abundance. Accompanied by the artillery, Prince Louis proceeded to
the barracks, the troops in which were entirely
ignorant of, and therefore unprepared for, the
presence of a pretender. Amongst the old soldiers
of the Empire the Prince was favourably received,
and their defection had a powerful influence on the
younger portion of the troops who knew the Empire
only .as a glorious tradition. A report, however,
spread amongst them that the whole affair was a
cheat, and that the Prince was only the nephew or
the son of Colonel Vaudrey. A lieutenant seized
the Prince, and that act dispersed the illusions of
Napoleonism. The artillery corps hesitated ; and
in such moments hesitation is defeat. Although

another artillery corps (the third) soon arrived on the spot to support the movement, when it became known that the Prince was a prisoner, his partisans dispersed, and each one looked to his personal safety. The majority were made prisoners ; but some escaped, amongst whom was the Prince's friend and constant adherent through all his fortunes, M. de Persigny, afterwards the Due de Persigny. The failure of this attempt brought little but ridicule to the Prince and his adherents ; and his best friends thought at the time that it had nearly extinguished all future hopes in the same direction. Louis Napoleon, however, was not to be so easily cast down ; he simply resolved to "bide his time."

The French Government now had Louis Napoleon fairly in their power, but how to dispose of him was their great difficulty. To deal with him as a traitor to the Government and to the dynasty might have proved an awkward example in the case of a monarch who owed his own throne to a revolution, and who began to be anything but liked by the French democracy of 1836. The Chamber of Peers were reluctant to try the case, and in the then temper of the people a trial by the ordinary process of jury might not have answered the expectations of the Government. Accordingly, after having been kept in the fortress of St. Louis at Strasburg till the 9th of November, Louis Napoleon was brought into Paris at night, where he was kept under guard, for two hours only ; being then sent off to Lorient, where he was placed on board a

vessel bound for America. Though he asked for a
trial in public court, he addressed a letter of thanks
to the King, which was regarded by the Government
as a kind of engagement that he would make no
further attempt to disturb public order. The
prosecution which was afterwards instituted against
his partisans and friends at Strasburg produced
a strong impression in that city and throughout the
whole of France. They were acquitted by the jury,
and the verdict was received with joy by all shades
of the Opposition as a check to the Government.

Louis Napoleon, however, did not remain long
in America. Having been informed that his mother
was dangerously ill, he hastened back to Europe.
The French Ambassador in London having refused
him a passport to go through France, he proceeded
to Switzerland by another route, where he found
Queen Hortense in a hopeless state. She died two
months afterwards, on the 3rd of October, 1837.
He had returned to Europe, as became a son, in
the hope of seeing Hortense once more, and (as he
says himself) of being allowed to close his mother's
dying eyes. Happily he came back in time to
perform this last office of filial duty. Unhappy
Hortense! "the flower of the Napoleons, as she has
deservedly been called ;" she passed her last years
in forced exile, far from the son who was her only
blessing, her only hope ; little suspecting-so far
as the outer world can judge-what a brilliant
destiny hereafter was awaiting her son ; for little
did she dream, as she lay on her bed of sickness,

and, as it proved, her death-bed, in her Swiss castle, that the same Louis Napoleon her son, who had been expelled from France along with herself by the Bourbonists as a child, and still more rudely and cruelly by the Orleanists when a man, would hereafter be enthroned in Paris and crowned in Notre-Dame as an emperor, while both Bourbons and Orleanists were pining away in foreign lands, exiles against their will, and the victims of their own selfish and illiberal policy.

Having paid the last rites to his mother, he appears to have resolved henceforth to look on the Swiss lakes and mountains as his adopted home.

Already, as far back as the years 1832-33, he had established his reputation as an original thinker and writer by the publication of his " Reveries Politiques," to which he appended the outline of a Constitution, in many respects greatly resembling that which he was afterwards mainly instrumental in bestowing upon France. In this work (says the author of the tract published by Messrs. Chambers), "After declaring that 'the end of the Republic was to establish the reign of equality and liberty;' that 'the nature of the Empire was to consolidate a throne based on the principles of the Revolution, to heal the wounds of France, and to regenerate the people ;' while 'its passions were love of country, love of glory, love of honour ;' he goes on to avow his strong conviction that the secret of the regeneration of France is to be found in a 're-combination of the two popular causes of the day

-that of the Empire and that of the Republic.' He adds-and it must be remembered that when he wrote, the King of Rome still lived-' the son of the first Napoleon is the sole representative of the highest amount of glory; just as the Republic is the embodiment of the greatest amount of natural liberty.'"

Proceeding to explain his principles, he thus appeals to the memories of the Empire and of his uncle the Emperor :-" Frenchmen ! let us not be unjust ; let us be grateful to him who, coming from amongst the ranks of the people, did everything for their well-being; who spread abroad the light of intelligence, and secured the independence of the country. If, one of these days, the people of France should become free, it is to Napoleon that they will owe it. He it was who habituated men to virtuous actions, the only sure basis of a republic. Do not reproach him for his dictatorial power ; it was that which led to freedom, as the iron plough which breaks the clods prepares the fertility of the soil. It was he who brought true civilisation to the world, from the Tagus to the Vistula ; it was he who implanted in the mind of France the principles of the Republic-equality before the laws, the superior claims of merit, the prosperity of commerce and industry, the enfranchisement of all nations- these were the objects to which he led us onward. . . . The misfortune of the Emperor Napoleon was, that he was not able to reap all that he had sown-that, havin~ delivered France, he was unable to leave her free." He follows up these remarks by suggesting that while, as respecting the government of France, every Frenchman has an ideal of his own, all should unite in trying to ascertain what is the will and the conviction of the people at large, who, in his judgment, are, in their collective capacity, the best and the only judges of their own destinies. He concludes by saying : "Let, then, all true Republicans and all true Napoleonists unite before the altar of their country to ascertain the will of the people."

It is impossible not to sympathise in such noble sentiments as these, and not to admire the man who could give them utterance while living in forced exile from that " native land " whose rulers scorned and spurned him, and under the strong - temptation of sharing an ancient throne like that of Portugal, and obtaining a home for himself and his mother on the banks of Tagus. But no; it was not to be : he had faith in that which some call "fortune," others " providence," and others "destiny ;" and he was contented to bide the issue of a future day, however long that day might be in coming. He would belong to France, and to France alone: on that he had made up his mind; but whether as a citizen or a soldier, a subject or a ruler, that was a secret as yet in the womb of time. He would wait, yes, even in exile, till it came to the birth. Not that he felt himself in any way bound to abstain from taking such measures as would hasten on the day when that secret should come to

the light.   With this object in view, he took part,
as has been related, in what was called at the time
the "Affair   of Strasburg;" with the same object
in view, some four years later, he made his abortive
descent upon the French   coast at Boulogne.   But
I must not anticipate the order of events.

CHAPTER V.

LOUIS NAPOLEON: HIS EXILE.

THE Prince continued to reside in Switzerland till the year 1838, when he found himself compromised in the eyes of the French King and his Ministry by an indiscreet publication by one of his adherents relating to the " affair of Strasburg," which served to keep the Prince's name before the public, and which was said to have been published with the "concurrence" of the Prince himself. The author of the book, Lieutenant Laity,* was brought before the Chamber of Peers, and, in spite of an able defence by M. Michel (of Bourges) was condemned to five years' imprisonment and a fine of 400/. ; whilst the French Government, not content with punishing the writer, followed up their triumph by a pressing demand to the Helvetic

---

* It may be interesting to learn that M. Laity was not forgotten when Louis Napoleon had the power of serving those who aided him in the perilous adventure of his early years. When the Prince was elected president of the Republic, M. Laity was reinstated in his position in the army. In 1854 he was made Prefect of the Bas Pyrenees, and Senator in 1857; he was likewise made a Commander of the Legion of Honour in 1855.

Confederation for the expulsion of the illustrious exile who had made Switzerland his home. The Swiss refused to give up their citizen, and were even ready to support their refusal by taking up arms in his defence; but rather than be a party to any step which should entail war-especially against a far stronger Power-on a people who had given him an hospitable asylum for so many years, Napoleon resolved at once upon quitting Arenenberg and coming to England.

Arrived in this country, he took up his abode in London, where he mixed much in general society. Here he gained many firm and fast friends, not merely on account of the name which he bore and the cause with which that name was identified, but mainly because they admired his unconquerable spirit, and devotion, and self-denial, and saw in him the promise of future greatness. From the following extract from a letter which, about this time, he addressed to a friend in France, it is clear that even during his residence in London he had never wholly abandoned those aspirations and patriotic ambitions which he had so fondly cherished whilst dwelling among the mountains of Switzerland:-

" You will be asked, as already some of the newspapers begin to ask, where is the Napoleonite party ? Reply to this : ' The party is nowhere, but the cause everywhere.' The party is nowhere, because my friends have not mustered; but the cause has partisans everywhere, from the workshop of the artisan to the council-chamber of the King ; from the barrack of the soldier to the palace of the marshal of France. Legitimists, Republicans, disciples of the *Juste milieu,* all who wish to see strong government and constitutional liberty, an imposing attitude on the part of authority-all these, I say, are Napoleonists, whether they avow it or not. • . • Perhaps, even yet, if, accustomed as they have been to despise authority, my countrymen should undermine the foundations of the social system, the name of Napoleon may prove an anchor of safety for all that is noble and worthy and serviceable in France."

While resident in London, not only did the Prince devote much time to a careful study of the English Constitution, both in theory and practice, but he took care to mix with men of thoughtful and philosophic minds, both English and foreign, and by this means gleaned much valuable information which those holding the highest position in the land must of necessity be precluded from obtaining. It was in London, likewise, that he formed those views of political philosophy of which he largely availed himself in his later published works, and especially in his "ldees Napoleoniennes==-a work which was first issued in a collective form in 1839.

From the middle of 1838, down to the month of August, 1840, Louis Napoleon continued to live among us, imbibing those amicable feelings which he ever afterwards cherished, both as President of the Republic and as head of the Empire of France, towards the country which extended to him its hospitality and protection when exiled and hunted

from the land of his adoption.   Here he did not
spend his time in indolence ; still less did he make
use of it in order to take note of our weak points,
that he might hereafter profit by his knowledge of
them.   On the contrary, he appears merely to have
mingled in general society with but little reserve,
and to have endeavoured to gain that stand-point
from which he could best take an appreciative view
of our laws, customs, and institutions.   He was to
be seen at our theatres, operas, and concerts, and
on our race-courses;   and in the autumn of 1839, he
played his part, as one of the contending knights,
in the revival of that display of medireval chivalry,
the Eglinton Tournament, in Scotland.

On August   6, 1840, with but little preparation
and concerted action, and attended   only by Count
Montholon and General Voison, and a few faithful
adherents, Louis Napoleon ventured upon an enterprise which ended more disastrously than the insurrection at Strasburg-nothing   less than a hostile
invasion of France.   He hired a small steamer, and,
crossing over to Boulogne from the English coast,
landed with his small band of followers on the shore
of France, and marched at once through the town
to the guard-house, shouting the well-remembered
cry of" Vive l'Empereur !" and distributing a few
copies of a printed proclamation which announced
a change in the Government.   The   soldiers were
called upon to join the Prince's standard; but, a
doubt having been raised as to the identity of the
newly-landed stranger with the nephew of the great

Napoleon-as was the case at Strasburg-the main body of the soldiers, with their officers, refused to follow his lead. The Prince, therefore, retreated towards the column of Napoleon, and there planted the Imperial flag. Here he soon found himself all but hemmed in by the soldiers and gendarmes, and therefore thought it prudent to attempt beating another retreat. It was, however, too late to make good his escape to the boat from which he had landed ; accordingly, without much difficulty, and with the loss of only one or two lives, the Prince and his two comrades were taken prisoners, and hurriedly conveyed to Paris. Louis Philippe very naturally would not allow this second blow at his power to pass unheeded, and the invaders were ordered to be brought to trial on a charge of high treason before the Chamber of Peers.

The prosecution of the Prince and his friends was conducted in a harsh and severe manner by the law officers of the Government, who were resolved to resort to *every* means in order to ensure a conviction. The Prince was defended by M. Berryer ; and when called on for his defence, he avowed that he, and he alone, was responsible for the abortive effort which he had made to ascertain the will of the French people with respect to the Empire, and to give them an opportunity of replying to the question: "Republic or Monarchy? the Empire or a Monarchy?" and of recovering for France her lost place in the scale of European nations. Notwithstanding M. Berryer's* eloquence in pleading the cause of the Prince, it is almost needless to say that he and his companions were found guilty. Count Montholon was sentenced to twenty years' imprisonment ; a young officer who had responded to Napoleon's call, to transportation; whilst the Prince himself was doomed to imprisonment for life, the Chateau of Ham, in Picardy, being fixed upon as the place of his incarceration.

It was towards the close of the year 1840, that Louis Napoleon found himself an inmate of the gloomy fortress of Ham; but his time here was not to be wasted in idle regrets. He spent it in the work of self-education, and in preparing himself for the destiny which, as he continued to believe,

---

* The following is the letter of thanks which the Prince addressed on this occasion to the eloquent advocate who had conducted his defence:-" My dear M. Berryer,-I cannot leave my Paris prison without again thanking you for the noble services you have rendered me during my trial. From the moment I knew that I was to be brought before the Court of Peers I had the idea of asking you to defend me, because I knew that the independence of your character would place you above the petty susceptibilities of party, and that your heart was open to every unfortunate, and your mind capable of understanding all grand ideas and noble feelings. I therefore chose you from esteem ; now I leave you with gratitude and friendship. I am ignorant of what fate may have in store for me, whether I shall ever be able to prove to you my gratitude, or whether you would accept any proof; but whatever be our reciprocal positions, putting politics and its desolating obligations aside, we can always hold each other in esteem and friendship, and I confess to you that if my trial had no other result than that of winning your friendship, I should still consider myself a great gainer, and should not complain of my lot. Adieu, my dear M. Berryer, and receive the assurance of my esteem and gratitude. "Louis NAPOLEON."

still awaited him; indeed, he would frequently say
to his friends that he had been " a student in the
hard school of necessity," and had "graduated at
the University of Ham"! He therefore accepted
his fate, if not with content, at all events with
dignity, declaring that the knowledge that he
was breathing the air of France and treading its
soil would be ample solace in his solitude. He
employed himself in various pursuits-in writing
letters. to Count d'Orsay and to Lady Blessington-
in cultivating a small garden, and in other ways
worthy of one who had ever looked to political
science as his *rtl/e,* and who, even in a prison, was
far from abandoning the hopes and aspirations
which belonged to a great cause. He also em·
ployed part of his time in prison in writing
pamphlets on the "Cultivation of Sugar," the
" Extinction of Pauperism," and the "Nicaraguan
Canal," and also a work entitled "Fragments
H istoriq ues."

Two, three, four years passed by, and still Louis
Napoleon continued in his imprisonment. During
this time he more than once received intimations of
a pardon if he were willing to accept the conditions
upon which it would be granted-namely, quitting
France, and abandoning his pretensions and claims;
but, rather than deign to accept such offers, he
looked upon them as insults. His feelings upon
the point are clearly indicated in the following lines
which he wrote to a friend at this time:-

" If to-morrow the doors of my prison were to be

opened to me, and I were told, 'You are free ; come and seat yourself as a citizen amid the hearths of your native country-France no longer repudiates her children,' ah ! then indeed a lively feeling of joy would seize my soul. But, if, on the contrary, they were to come to off~r me to exchange my present condition for that of an exile, I should refuse such a proposition, because it would be in my view an aggravation of punishment. I prefer being a captive on the soil of France, to being a free man in a foreign land. In a word, I should repeat-supposing that the occasion pre-sented itself to me-that which I declared before the Court of Peers-' I will not accept of generosity, because I know how much it costs.' "

During his confinement one voice was raised for mercy on his behalf, and that voice came from England. The late Marquis of Londonderry had known both the Monarch and the State prisoner in former days, and he addressed a memorial to Louis Philippe, praying that some remission of the sentence might be accorded to the prisoner. It was not likely that this application would have had any effect; the French king was, probably, too afraid of his prisoner lightly to let him out of his grasp, and the prayer of the memorial was curtly, not to say even rudely, refused.

In 1845 he applied to the French Government for permission to visit his father, the ex-King of Holland, who was then lying dangerously ill at Florence, his solicitation being accompanied by a promise to return to his prison on receiving notice from the Government ; but this request was peremptorily refused by Louis-Philippe, except upon terms by which the Prince at once declined to be bound. This refusal, it may be added, gained for him at least one advantage-a knowledge of the true position in which he stood to Louis-Philippe, and a feeling that henceforth there must be uncompro, mising war between the Imperial name and the House of Orleans. In the following May (1846), the Prince's desire to see his father before he died led him to meditate an escape from the durance of his prison. Assisted by Dr. Conneau, a fellow-prisoner, devoted to his interests, and a faithful servant, Charles Thelier, Louis Napoleon was enabled to carry this design into execution on the 25th of the above month. How the escape was effected the Prince has himself thus described in a letter to M. de George :-

" You know," he writes, "that the fort was guarded by 400 men, who furnished daily 60 soldiers, placed as sentries outside the walls. Moreover, the principal gate of the prison was guarded by three gaolers, two of whom were constantly on duty. It was necessary that I should first elude their vigilance, afterwards traverse the inside court before the windows of the commandant's residence, and arriving there, I should be obliged to pass by a gate which was guarded by soldiers. Not wishing to communicate my design to any one, it was necessary to disguise myself. As several rooms in

that part of the prison which I occupied were under
repair, it was not difficult to assume the dress of a
workman.   My good and faithful valet, Charles
Thelier, procured a smock-frock and a pair of
sabots ; and, after shaving off my moustaches, I
took a plank on my shoulders.   On Sunday morning I saw the workmen enter at half-past eight
o'clock.   Charles took them some drink, in order
that I should not meet any of them on my way.
He was also to call one of the turnkeys, whilst Dr.
Conneau with the others.   Nevertheless,
I had scarcely got out of my room before I was
accosted by a workman, who took me for one of his
comrades ; and at the bottom of the stairs I found
myself in front of the keeper.   Fortunately, I
placed before my face the plank which I was
carrying, and succeeded in reaching the yard.
Whenever I passed a sentinel or any other person,
I always kept the plank before my face.   Passing
before the first sentinel, I let my pipe fall, and
stopped to pick up the bits.   There I met the
officer on duty ; but as he was reading a letter he
paid no attention to me.   The soldiers at the
guard-house appeared surprised at my dress, and a
chasseur turned round several times to look at me.
I next met some workmen, who looked very atten-
tively at me.   I placed the plank before my face,
but they appeared to be so curious that I thought
I should never escape until I heard them say, 'Oh,
it is Bertrand !'   Once outside, I walked quickly
towards the road to St. Quentin.   Charles, who

had the day before engaged a. carriage, shortly overtook *me,* and we arrived at St. Quentin. I passed through the town on foot, after having thrown off my smock-frock. Charles procured a post-chaise, under pretext of going to Cambrai. We arrived, without meeting any obstacles, at Valenciennes, where I took the railway. I had procured a Belgian passport, but I was nowhere asked to show· it. During my escape, Dr. Conneau, always so devoted to me, remained in prison, and caused them to believe that I was unwell, in order to give me time to reach the frontier. Before I could be persuaded to quit France, it was necessary that I should be convinced that the Government would never set me at liberty if I would not consent to dishonour myself. It was also a matter of duty that I should exert all my efforts in order to be enabled to solace my father in his old age."

It is scarcely possible to speak too highly of the Prince's medical attendant, Dr. Conneau, who, by feigning the continued illness of his illustrious patient, had thus gained for him time to make good his retreat beyond the French frontiers, whilst he himself remained within the fortress, ready to bear his share of punishment for complicity in the escape of his charge, when he, *too,* probably, might have walked out free. It is true he was tried for his offence, but was acquitted.

Having reached the Belgian frontier, the Prince lost not a moment in taking ship for England, and on the first of *June,* the first Monday after his escape from Ham, he was at the St. James's Theatre, witnessing the performance of the French actors. The immediate object of the Prince's escape-that of seeing his venerable parent once more before he died-was frustrated; for the French Government had the meanness to instruct the Austrian Ambassador (who likewise represented Tuscany at St. James's) to refuse him the necessary passports. Thus, for the third time, Napoleon found an asylum in England, and here he continued to reside for nearly another two years, dividing his time between London and a country house which he had hired at Brasted, near Sevenoaks, in Kent, patiently waiting the turn in the wheel of fortune which should bring him once more to that native land to which his thoughts were always directed.

CHAPTER VI.

THE PRESIDENT.

IN the month of February, 1848, the opportunity for which the Prince had so long waited was suddenly brought about by the overthrow of the Government of Louis-Philippe, after a few hours of insurrection by the people whom that administration had failed to conciliate, and the King himself was only too glad to effect his escape in disguise to the coast, and to land as an exile* on the very shores to which in effect he had consigned the Prince whom he considered as the most formidable rival of his throne. Notwithstanding that the sentence of proscription against himself and his family was still unrepealed, the revolution had scarcely broken out when Louis Napoleon left London and hurried to Paris, where he at once proceeded to pay his respects to the Provisional Government, such as it was. Finding, however, that his presence was likely

* Like Louis Napoleon himself, Louis-Philippe died an exile in England, in 1850. He lies buried temporarily at Weybridge, in Surrey, an inscription on his tomb declaring that his remains rest there " donec in patriam transferantur."

to prove an embarrassment, he withdrew from the city and returned to London, where in the following April he gave a new pledge of his opposition to the views of the friends of anarchy, and of his own support of order and law, by enrolling himself as a special constable on an occasion when it was expected that the peace would be broken in the streets of London by organised bands of agitators. A proposal was shortly afterwards made in the National Assembly of France to repeal the proscription against the Bonaparte family, with the single exception of the Prince himself. This led to a strong protest from the Prince, who wrote to the "citizen representatives" to know the cause of this invidious distinction ; at the same· time adding :-
" The same reasons which have made me ere this take up arms against the Government of Louis Philippe would lead me, if my services were required, to devote myself to the defence of the Assembly, as being the result of universal suffrage.

In the presence of the national sovereignty I cannot and will not claim more than my rights as a French citizen; but these. I will ever demand with an energy which an honest heart must desire, from the knowledge that it has never done anything to render it unworthy of its country."

In spite of this personal drawback the Prince was, in September, 1848, elected a representative in the National Assembly by five different departments, and by such emphatic majorities that it was impossible any longer to enforce the proscription against him. He accordingly took his seat in the Assembly on the 26th of the same month ; and as the Provisional Government no longer inspired respect, and the multitude clamoured for a President, it was resolved that one should be chosen. The candidates for this high office were General Cavaignac, M. Ledru-Rollin, Louis Napoleon Bonaparte, M. Raspail, M. de Lamartine, and General Changarnier. The choice of the people, whose votes were given by universal suffrage, fell on Louis Napoleon by an overwhelming majority, and on the roth of December, 1848, he was proclaimed " President of the French Republic from this day until the second Sunday of May, 1852." He took the oath of fidelity on the zoth of December, after which he addressed the Assembly in these words :-" The suffrages of the nation and the oath I have just taken command my future conduct. My duty is clearly traced out : I will fulfil it as a man of honour. I shall regard as the enemies of the country all who seek to change by illegal means that which entire France has established. . . I desire, in common with yourselves, citizen representatives, to consolidate society upon its true basis, to establish democratic institutions, and earnestly to devise the means calculated to relieve the sufferings of the generous and intelligent people who have just bestowed on me so signal a proof of their confidence."

In his new capacity as President of the new Republic he did not conceal his own opinion that the

Imperial system with an Imperial head was the best system for France. But he had found a Republican form of Government established, and his desire being that this form should be administered in its integrity, irrespective of factions and parties, he plainly told the Assembly that this result never would or could be attained unless the person entrusted with the chief authority should be honestly and heartily supported by the leading members of their body.

With him to think and to propound was also to act, as he showed by his. next political step, the famous *coup d'etat,* the story of which is thus told by a writer in the *Mornz"ng Post* :-

" On the morning of the znd of December, 185 r, stimulated by the urgent advice and aided by the energetic action of such men as St. Arnaud and Fleury, Napoleon made his famous *coup d'etat.* On the previous night he had held a grand reception at the Elysee, and when the citizens of Paris awoke in the morning they found a presidential decree posted on the walls announcing the step which had been taken, and also proclamations addressed to the people calling on them to affirm or negative the step. The Assembly was declared to be dissolved and universal suffrage re-established. In his address to the nation the President said :-

" ' Persuaded that the instability of the Government and the preponderance of a single Assembly are permanent causes of trouble and disorder, I submit to your will the following basis of a constitution :- I. A responsible head, named for two years. 2. Ministers dependent on the executive power alone. 3. A council of state formed of the most eminent men, preparing the laws, and supporting the discussion of them before the legislative body. 4. A legislative body discussing and voting laws, and to be nominated by universal suffrage without *scrutis. de lisle,* which falsifies the election. 5. A second Assembly, formed of all the eminent men in the country, a preponderating power, guardian of the fundamental compact and of public liberties. The system founded by the First Consul at the commencement of the century has already given to France repose and prosperity, and it would again guarantee them to it. Such is my profound conviction. If you share in it, declare it by your suffrages. If, on the contrary, you prefer a government without strength, Monarchical or Republican, borrowed from I know not what past, or from some chimerical future, reply negatively. Thus, then, for the first time since 1804, you will vote with a knowledge of what you are doing, knowing well for whom and what. If I do not obtain the majority of your suffrages, I will then call for the meeting of a new Assembly, and I will give up the charge which I have received from you. But if you believe that the cause, of which my name is the symbol-that is to say, France regenerated by the Revolution of 1789, and organised by the Emperor -is still your own, proclaim it by consecrating the powers which I ask from you. Then will Franee and Europe be preserved from anarchy ; obstacles will be removed, rivalries will have disappeared, for all will respect, in the decision of the people, the decree of Providence:

" Before sunrise on that eventful morning every statesmen of the hostile faction was arrested and imprisoned ; a number of picked regiments were marched into the streets to repress all opposition ; and then, having possessed himself of every element of power, he offered himself to France for ten years' election to the office of President, with constitutive power. He was returned, and he afterwards proclaimed a Constitution which gave absolute power to himself. The Ministry was to be responsible to him only; he was to have command of the land and sea forces, and was to declare war or a state of siege on his own authority. The verdict of the nation at large upon the important measures which the President had found it necessary to take for the interests of the country was taken by universal suffrage. The votes, which were taken by ballot, on the zoth and arst of December, 1851, showed that the *coup d'etat* was approved by a very large majority, namely 7,439,219 against 640,737.

The story of the *coup d'eta!* is told, from a very different point of view, by a writer in *Reyuolds's Newspaper:-*" He who had sworn before the Assembly and the world to defend the Constitution, was the person to plot, in secret and deliberately, its overthrow. In the middle of the night were arrested General~ Cavaignac, Changarnier, Lamori ..

ciere, Leflo, Bedeau, Colonel Charras, Messrs.
C. Lagrange, Greppo, Baze, Thiers, &c. The
official historian relates that M. Thiers exhibited
' great consternation ' when the police commissary
drew aside the curtains of crimson damask and
informed him that he was a prisoner, and that his
courage entirely forsook him when in prison.
General Changarnier was taken in his bed-room,
'in his shirt, barefoot, and a pistol in either hand.'
General Cavaignac ' showed signs of exasperation
-he smote with his clenched fist upon a marble
table, and vented his wrath in a volley of abuse.'
General Larnoriciere, when he heard the noise in
his house, very naturally shouted, 'Thieves, thieves!'
and when on his way to Mazas he put his head out
of the carriage and attempted to harangue the
troops. General Leflo also endeavoured to address
the troops as he stepped into the carriage, but was
soon compelled to silence by Colonel Espinasse.
Colonel Charras said, ' I expected this ; had you
come two days earlier I would have blown your
brains out. Are you taking me to be· shot?'
Several others, besides the representatives of the
people, were arrested, but they were not treated
with the same consideration. The National
Assembly was surrounded and taken possession of
by half-past six. Some of the deputies, however,
found their way into the chamber, but orders were
issued for their immediate dispersion. The president, Dupin, said, ' Gentlemen, the Constitution is
violated ; right is on our side, but might is against

us. I recommend you to retire and have the
honour to bid you farewell.' No less than 220
deputies, under the presidency of M. Benoit d'Azy,
decreed the fall of the President ; M. Berryer read
the decree from the window ; the command of the
troops and National Guard was assigned to General
Oudinot and General Lauriston ; the High Court
of Justice was also called together, and Louis
Napoleon was 'pronounced guilty of high treason.'
But these measures were ' too late.' The magis-
trates and the deputies were dispersed by troops
who were prepared, and, by nightfall of the znd
December, 217 deputies of France were lodged
in the prisons Mazas, Mont Valerien, and Vin·
cennes.

"On December 4th, Paris passed through a
terrible crisis. To the men then in command,
Marshals St. Arnaud and Magnan, the shedding of
blood was a matter of small moment. 'Don't be
uneasy,' said General Magnan to the Minister of
War ; 'trust me with the management of matters
to-day, ·and I'll answer for the result. At two
o'clock you'll hear the roar of my cannon; and I
promise you that with such troops as these Paris
will be rid of its enemies by nightfall.' ' I expect
as much,' said St. Arnaud, 'and I₄ leave everything
at your own disposal, for I know you well.' The
roar of cannon was soon heard, Bourgon's brigade
opened fire and swept the Boulevard as far as the
Porte St. Denis ; Reybell's brigade swept the Boulevard from the Madeleine to the Boulevard Mont-

martre.   After reaching the upper part of the
Boulevard Montmartre, without striking a blow, it
suddenly halted, and seconded by sharpshooters
and troops from Canrobert's brigade, opened a
terrible fire upon the windows, burst open the doors
with cannon shot, and drove out the insurgents
after having put to death a considerable number of
them.   Only 25 of the troops were killed and 181
wounded.   How many of the people fell can never
be ascertained, but whole heaps of slain lay
dead," and were carted off to the cemeteries for
burial."

" Six years of imprisonment did not quench Louis
Napoleon's passion for sovereign power.   During
that period his naturally reflective disposition led
him to review his chances, and study the means of
securing the aim of his life.   But when he landed
in England from Belgium he earnestly proclaimed
his pacific resolves, and asserted the purity of his
intentions.   Thus once again he was in exile; but
being a free man, he was in a position to act, should
the fitting opportunity arrive.   It came two years
after his escape.   Louis Philippe in 1847 had for-
feited the confidence of his subjects, and in February. 1848, the throne yielded to the slightest
push from the tumultuous Parisians.   Louis-Philippe
fled to England, and France became a Republic.
Here was an opening not likely to be neglected by
the aspiring Prince.   He went to Paris, but was
requested to withdraw, and again betook himself
into exile.   But in June he was elected to !he

Constituent Assembly. Three months afterwards he was elected by five constituencies, and was allowed to take his seat; but he had a slight share in th- business work, and voted only four times. His presence in Paris and in the Assembly raised a larger question. A President was to be elected in December, and his name at once went to the front rank. General Cavaignac, at that time the actual head of the Government, was his competitor; but he secured less than a million and a half of votes, while Prince Louis saw himself the chosen nominee of 5,552,834 Frenchmen. When the votes cast for Louis Napoleon came to be scrutinised, some curious discoveries were made, showing how little many of his supporters knew of him personally, but how fanatically they clung to the phantom of the first empire. The new President formed a ministry, and sought to govern by and with the Assembly.

"But conflicts soon rose between the legislative and executive powers. The Assembly desired to govern the President and the President sought to rule the Assembly. The contest was continued on divers subjects throughout the year 1849. The President's notions of his duties did not accord with those of the Assembly ; and the President, while holding his own in the cabinet, turned his attention to the army, and secured the devotion of the generals and soldiers. Towards the end of 1851 the Assembly felt that it was engaged in a conflict for existence, and rumours of a *coup d'etat* were common ; but that body, tom by dissensions, and forming the scene of passionate debates, had not the skill or the courage to take adequate defensive measures.

"At the end of November the Imperialist plot was ripe. On the znd of December, 185 I, Paris was placarded with a presidential decree dissolving the Legislative Body. The proclamation was set up at the dead of night by the compositors in the govern. ment printing-office, a gendarme standing behind each workmen. Directly afterwards warrants were handed to a bevy of commissaries of police in waiting; and, by the orders of the President, a host of members of the Assembly were arrested in their beds and flung into prison. The politicians thus kidnapped included General de Lamoriciere and M. Thiers. The latter was, after a few days' detention, politely conducted over the frontier, by the Bridge of Kehl, into Germany. The veteran statesman had to pass into exile through that Strasbourg which had been the scene of Louis Napoleon's first and abortive attempt to seize upon power; and eighteen years after the *coup d'etat* the Germans were bombarding Strasbourg and wresting it from defeated and distracted France.

" The seizure of the representatives of the people being consummated, the troops, commanded by St. Arnaud, occupied Paris in force. A large number of deputies assembled and declared themselves *en permanence,* but were driven off by soldiers. The High Court of Justice met and declared the President guilty of high treason, but the troops dissolved the court before the decree could be signed. The action of the President and his agents was completely successful ; but the success was gravely marred by those massacres in the streets, the precise origin of which has never been ascertained. The *coup d'etat* was an act of violence ably conceived and unflinchingly executed, and it secured the President in the possession of absolute power.

" He devised a fresh constitution suited to his own notions of absolute personal government. He took a vote or plebiscite on the doings of the znd December; and 7,500,000 Frenchmen readily confirmed his conduct, and gave him authority to rule for ten years, instead of holding his office, as heretofore, by annual re-election. In the beginning of 1852 decrees fell in showers on the country, whose institutions were again remodelled. A senate sprung up, a legislative body, a council of state. The press was placed in the strictest fetters. But on the whole France was satisfied ; stocks rose ; order was secured ; and a new era of speculation dawned upon the country. A year afterwards, again on the znd of December, the Prince President had the gratification of obtaining a fresh popular vote, which, by millions as before, ratified his transition from the headship of a nominal republic to the imperial throne. Four years after he landed in France as a deputy, he corresponded with crowned heads as Napoleon III., and began a reign memorable in French history for a host of brilliant suecesses-not obliterated even by the tempestuous and destructive climax of Sedan."

The *Times* thus briefly and pithily sums up in general terms the account of this measure with which the Emperor's name will be for ever linked in history :-" From the beginning of 1851 everything was being made ready for a final conflict. Early in January, Changarnier was removed from his command. To insure the continuance of his power, he resolved on the *coup d'etat* of the and of December. He laid a violent hand on his most dreaded opponents. He dispersed the less dangerous. He dissolved the Assembly and the Council of State. He abrogated the law of May 31, and re-established, universal suffrage. He then called together the 'Comitia of the nation.' In the meantime, he declared Paris in a state of siege; he deluged its streets with blood ; he terrorised France by wholesale transportation. He finally asked for a sanction or condemnation of his deed of violence. Seven millions and a half of Frenchmen against little above half a million gave sentence in his favour."

It cannot and it need not be denied that very many sensible and well-informed persons have severely censured Louis Napoleon for his policy in making this *coup d'etat,·* but, whatever may be thought of its intrinsic character, it must be allowed that it was justified by necessity. The choice, as a matter of fact, lay at the moment between the strong rule of a single individual

F

or an outbreak of Socialism, accompanied by the
horrors and misdeeds of the vile "Commune,"
with which we have since been made so un-
happily familiar. It is clear to those who take
into account the actual circumstances in which the
Prince President was placed that he was driven to
that step by the imperative necessity of a very
simple alternative. Montalembert, who was anything but a Bonapartist, and who, as a lover of Constitutional Government, was almost as truly a loyal
Englishman as he was certainly a patriotic French-
-man, shall pronounce as to the nature of that
necessity. On the morrow of the *coup d'etat* the
Count de Montalembert wrote, avowedly in his own
name, in the columns of the *Univers* :-" To vote
against Louis Napoleon would be to declare in
favour of a Socialist revolution. To vote at all is
to choose between him and the total ruin of France.
I seek in vain elsewhere for a system capable of
guaranteeing to us the preservation and development of the benefits which mark his government.
Elsewhere I see only the gaping gulf of victorious
Socialism." What was thought or declared thus by
the lips, or,- rather more deliberately, by the hand
of Montalembert, was thundered forth immediately
afterwards by the voices of more than seven millions of Frenchmen. Not merely that, but. nearly
eight millions raised him to the Imperial throne
within a year afterwards-as nearly as possible the
same vast majority approving his whole reign a
score of years after that, upon the very eve when,

by an unparalleled catastrophe, the fall of the Emperor was succeeded, after the closing agonies of the war of 1870, by the temporary ruin of Paris, if not of France, in *the gaping gulf of victorious Socialism !*

Shortly after the *coup d'etat,* petitions and memorials for the restoration of the Empire were received *by* the Assembly and its President from every Department and district, and, in order to ascertain the real state of popular feeling in the matter, in the autumn of 1852 the Prince President accordingly visited the southern Departments, and was everywhere most enthusiastically received. His return to Paris was of a no less cordial and demonstrative character, and deputations, memorials, and addresses followed him from nearly all the municipal bodies, demanding, with pressing unanimity, the restoration of the Empire. The proposal for the restoration was theu duly made and submitted to the nation, and decided in the affirmative by a majority of five or six million votes. The Empire was accordingly proclaimed on the 2nd of December following,the Prince assuming the style and title of "Napoleon III., Emperor of the French, by the grace of God and the will of the People."

According to a writer in the *Standard,* " The Empire thus vindicated and recognised abroad was no less firmly established at home. It was soon found that the union of Republican institutions with Imperial administration meant the exaltation

of the Empire to a maximum and the reduction of
the Republic to a minimum.   Universal suffrage
was declared to be the basis of the Government,
but after universal suffrage had restored the Empire
and proclaimed the Emperor he saw that there was
little else left for it to do.   The right of meeting
was forbidden.   The Press was subjected to ad-
ministrative control, which, though oppressive and
fatal to many journals, did not prevent publicists
like Prevost Paradol achieving a reputation second
only to that attained under the Restoration.   The
men of former dynasties stood aloof.   Napoleon
had, indeed, tlirown open the prison doors to most
of those whom he imprisoned in December, 185 I,
as soon as the crisis was over and the prize of
empire was in his grasp, but he could not win them
to his side.   The generals, the authors, the orators,
the thinkers of the former reigns formed coteries of
their own, while the Court was crowded by men
who had been adherents of Napoleon in his adversity, or early converts to his star.   It was necessary
that the Emperor should offer France some com-
pensation for the liberties of which he had deprived
her, and this was to be ,ound in the enormous
stimulus given to mercantile adventure and speculation, carried on in the most colossal proportions,
and at which Englishmen, who had heretofore
fancied themselves at the head of the commerce of
the world, looked with mixed feelings of envy and
apprehension.   The city of Paris especially was the
object of his care.   No expense was spared, no

consideration was allowed to interfere with the beautifying of a city which all Parisians regarded as the representative of France. Under the energetic rule of M. Haussmann the old narrow and tortuous lanes disappeared, and the city was traversed in its length and breadth by broad handsome streets and spacious boulevards, which were, however, viewed in some quarters-how groundlessly the Commune subsequently showed -as calculated to prevent all future street· fighting."

Through all the changing functions which he had assumed in these troublous times, Louis Napoleon was readily recognised by the English Government and by most of the continental powers. His resumption of the name, style, and title of Emperor, borne by his uncle, created a difficulty. It was a name that revived painful associations in many of the other countries of Europe. To them the Empire meant aggression, invasion, conquest, and spoliation-an enemy which it had once before required an united Europe to put down. And these suspicions were not allayed by the evident determination of the new Emperor to link his Empire in close connection with the old one, as was shown by his taking the title of Napoleon III. In other respects he did what he could to reassure the hearts, both of his own subjects and of other people, by his celebrated declaration that "the Empire was peace," in words which have since passed into a proverb. The English Government, as usual in all such cases, led the way in recognition of his Government ; afterwards the other Sovereigns followed, the last to move in the matter being the Emperor of Russia.

CHAPTER VII.

LOUIS NAPOLEON'S MARRIAGE AND THE CRIMEAN ,,.AR.

THE accession of the *parventt* and once-exiled Prince to the honours of an Imperial throne, and the restoration of a "court" at the Tuileries, was the signal to Paris to put on its gayest appearance, and balls, suppers, operas, &c., became the order of the day. The Paris correspondent of the *Guardian* at this time writes : "We now have Louis Napoleon, day by day, or, rather, night by night, dressed in white culottes with diamond buckles, and dancing with all his might. His whole court dances along with him : eight balls to be given by eight high functionaries in the next ten days are advertised in the papers. Splendour and adulation surround him on every side. He treads on silver, and is served on gold."

The new Emperor no sooner found himself fairly seated on the Imperial throne than he looked around him for an Empress able and willing to share it, together with all those vicissitudes of fortune to which the very highest personages are more exposed than others. And such a lady he found in Eugenie, Countess de Teba, who has proved herself the best, the bravest, and the most tenderly affectionate of wives. For nearly twenty years she graced· the court of the Tuileries as few women had done before her. Beautiful in person, and exquisite in taste, she became the leader of fashion in every capital; and in fair as well as in adverse fortune she has proved herself the truest and most loyal friend of her Imperial husband. This union very greatly enhanced his own popularity, and helped, doubtless, to establish the position of the *parvenu-as* he modestly styled himself-in the various courts of Europe. He lost no time in announcing his matrimonial intentions to his Cabinet.

She is of noble Spanish parentage, her father being a Montijo, but comes on her maternal grandfather's side of Scottish extraction; and, if we may believe a French genealogist, she is also descended from St. Louis, and so from the line of Capet. But these are points of lesser importance, when compared with her goodness of disposition and her personal bravery, which she displayed alike in visiting the cholera hospitals at Paris and Amiens and during her short regency in the month of August, 1870, during the first month of that unhappy war which cost her husband his throne.

Though of foreign birth and extraction, both she and her mother had spent some years in early life at Clifton in England, as well as at Malaga in Spain, where her maternal grandfather, named Fitzpatrick or Kirkpatrick, was a merchant and consul. Her father, the Count de Montijo, though Spanish by blood, was an officer in the French army, and was therefore one of the few Spanish gentlemen who were found among the invaders of his own country. " The French papers," observes a writer of the time, "dwell much upon this fact, and upon M. de Montijo's wounds at Salamanca, upon his participation in the campaign of 1814, and upon his co-operation in the defence of Paris, as matters of great honour and congratulation on the present occasion ; but in the eyes of his own countrymen such a career can surely be only regarded as the reverse of meritorious. Indeed, the subsequent success of the family at Madrid, after its succession to the grandeeship and its numerous titles, appears to have been mainly owing to the *sauoir faire* of Madame de Montijo, of whose clever manceuvring the present exaltation of her daughter affords no mean specimen, especially if the cause of her presence in Paris for the first time, as I believe this winter, and the errand upon which she at first professed to have come, have been rightly explained to me."

It is almost needless to add that the wedding of the Imperial pair was celebrated with all possible splendour and magnificence. The civil marriage having been gone through at the Tuileries on the previous evening, in the presence of the members of _b_?th_families, the religious ceremony was performed at Notre Dame on Sunday, January 30, 1853, with lavish magnificence, with salvos of artillery, and amid the congratulations of the whole Parisian populace. Every house was decorated along the streets between the Tuileries and the Cathedral, and all the windows, and hundreds of balconies and extemporized lines of seats, were filled with a gaily dressed crowd of well-wishers. Judging by the contemporary accounts which are to be found in the newspapers of the time, the wedding must have been a grand spectacle.

The clergy, headed by the Archbishop of Paris, entered the church about eleven, and at half-past the Papal Nuncio arrived, leading the Catholic diplomatic corps. A little before one, the signal of their Majesties' arrival being given by the great bell of the cathedral, the archbishop passed down the centre aisle, crosier in hand, wearing his mitre, and preceded by his cross-bearer, to meet them. At the great entrance the Archbishop offered to the Emperor and Empress a remnant of the true cross to kiss, as well as the holy water and incense, after which, four ecclesiastics holding over them a rich canopy, their Majesties proceeded to their places. The Bishop of Nancy, First Almoner, in his rochet and pallium, held the prayer-book of his Majesty, ready to hand on the commencement of the service, which, on a signal from the gran8 master of the ceremonies, the Archbishop first saluting their Majesties, forthwith began. The Emperor and Empress then, each holding the other's right hand, descended to the altar, and were thus addressed by the Archbishop :-"You appear here for the purpose of contracting marriage in the face of the Holy Church?" The Emperor and Empress replied, "Yes, Sir." After these words, the First Almoner left his place, preceded by a master of the ceremonies, and laid on the salver the pieces of gold and the ring, to receive the benediction of the Archbishop. The *piece de mariage,* as it is called, was of massive gold, set round the edge with diamonds, having on one side the cipher of Napoleon III. and that of Marie Eugenie de Guzman, and on the other, written in diamonds, the date of the marriage. After the benediction, the Archbishop thus addressed the Emperor :-" Sire, you declare, affirm, and swear, before God and in the face of His Holy Church, that you take for your lawful wife Mdlle. Eugenie de Montijo, Countess de Teba, here present?" The Emperor replied, "Yes, Sir." After repeating the first question to the Empress, the Archbishop continued, "You promise and swear to observe fidelity to him in every respect, as a faithful wife is bound to do, according to the commandment of God ? " The Empress replied, "Yes, Sir." The Archbishop then handed to the Emperor the pieces of gold and the ring ; and his Majesty presented the pieces of gold to the Empress, saying, " Receive the tokens of the matrimonial connection between you and me." The Emperor then placed the ring on the fourth finger of the Empress's left hand, saying, " I give you this ring as a symbol of the marriage which we are contracting." The Archbishop then making the sign of the Cross on the hands of the Empress, said, *"In nomin« Patri et Filii, et Spiritus Sancti."* The ceremony over, the Pontifical benediction fol. lowed, the choir chanting *Domine sahrum,* and finally, during the execution of the *Te Deum,* the Archbishop presented the *Corporate* to their Majesties to kiss. The cure of St. Germain l'Auxerrois, the parish church of the Tuileries, then presented for signature the parish register, which terminated the ceremony; and all hastened to resume their places in the procession, which returned in the same order in which it went. During the ceremony the Empress herself shed no tears, but her mother, the Comtesse de Montijo, is reported to have been much affected. The pro· cession returned along the quays to the Place de la Concorde, and entered the Tuileries garden from thence by what is called the *Pont tournant.* The crowd was by this time most dense along the whole line of route, and the royal carriage stopped several times to receive bouquets from the deputations, and from the children of various schools. On arriving at the Tuileries the Emperor and Empress appeared arm-in-arm on the centre balcony for a few moments, and also drove through the lines of troops drawn up in the court behind. In less than an hour afterwards the Emperor, in plain clothes, and the Empress, in morning bonnet and ermine cloak, left in a plain chariot and four horses for St. Cloud.

Four thousand persons, it is said, were amnestied on the occasion of the Emperor's marriage. The Municipal Council of Paris having assembled and voted 6oo,ooo francs (£24,000) for the purchase of a diamond necklace, to be presented to the Empress, in the name of the City of Paris, her Majesty, in a letter expressive of her gratitude for this mark of attachment, declined the proffered present, at the same time requesting that the sum voted for the purpose might be laid out on some charitable institution. The council decided that such an establishment should be forthwith founded, which should bear the name of the Empress. Twenty-eight young women were married and dowered on this auspicious occasion. A credit of 300,000 francs (£12,000) was placed at the disposal of the Prefect of the Seine for acts of charity, and for the liberation of tools, furniture, &c., from the different *monts-de-pilte.* Double rations of wine and soup were served out to all the troops, and all offences against discipline were amnestied.

The only issue of this marriage, as all the world is aware, is her son, the Prince Imperial, who was born at the Tuileries on the 16th of March, 185,.6, and was baptised, with all due form and pomp, by the names of Napoleon Eugene Louis Jean Joseph.

It is possible that the slowness of the Russian Emperor to acknowledge the French *parvenu* (as mentioned above) rankled in Napoleon's heart with a bitterness which, deeply as he felt it,"he was too proud to show, and that at a very early date he began to devise in his own mind plans for the purpose of making the Czar feel his mistake. What is known as "The Eastern Question" had slept for years, and might have slept on for a much longer time, if the newly-crowned Emperor had not thought of waking it up again. The following statement of facts is necessary in order to enable the reader to understand the real history and meaning of that Crimean War, which did so much to cement our friendship with him who is now deceased, and also less happily to reveal our own deficiencies, and the shortcomings of our army system as a whole, when compared with other countries. It came about in this way. The Church of the Holy Sepulchre at Jerusalem had been under the joint protection of France and Russia, as the representatives of the Latin and Greek Churches; but about this time it was discovered that the roof of the church was out of repair, and the French Emperor instructed his ambassador at Constantinople to assume the full control of the church, and on that assumption to proceed to have the church repaired at the French expense. Instantly the whole diplomatic world was astir. The part thus taken by France was precisely that which had always been assumed by Russia, though of late years she had tolerated the pretensions of the Latin Christians to joint possession; but to be thus shouldered out of her rights altogether was

too much, and she prepared to assert them at
the point of the bayonet. At this point England
and the other Powers interfered, and in the end
Louis Napoleon was induced to withdraw his
claims, while Russia recognised his government;
and the temple which the great majority of the
Christian world believed to stand over the sepulchre of the Prince of Peace was spared the scandal
of becoming the cause of a bloody war. And yet
the escape was little more than nominal. It was
really this quarrel over the Church of the Holy
Sepulchre that led to the Crimean war. For the
Emperor Nicholas, thoroughly aroused at this attempt to deprive him of that protection to the
Holy Places which was one main cause of the
veneration with which he was regarded by every
Oriental Christian, determined to put it effectually
out of the power of any Sovereign to interfere in
this way for the future. He advanced claims upon
Turkey, and demanded concessions from her which
could not have been conceded without surrendering ~
the integrity and independence of the Turkish
Empire. All the world knows the result. England, under the sway of Lord Aberdeen, the most
pacific of English Ministers, was proud of being
united in alliance with France, while the French
Emperor desired nothing better than that his new
Government and title should be strengthened by
an alliance with a settled government like that of
England. The result was the Crimean war, which
began in 1854, and was brought to a close early in

1856, when the English and French flags waved side by side in triumph over the ruined city of Sebastopol.

It must be candidly acknowledged, even by the late Emperor's enemies, that this war in which our own soldiers and his troops were linked together by the presence of a common enemy, did much to raise Louis Napoleon in the estimation not only of England but of other European Courts and Capitals.

It is still a matter of dispute whether the faults of the campaign were more attributable to the French or the English commanders, though the world is pretty well agreed that the evils of a divided command were never more signally illustrated ; but it is certain that on the Continent the French managed to carry off the lion's share of the glory, while the English were regarded as the great obstructions to progress and suceess. In the negotiations that followed the war our character came out to more advantage. It could not be concealed that Louis Napoleon would have closed the war even before the fall of Sebastopol but for the persistence of the English ; and when afterwards, in settling the terms of peace, negotiations arose as to the limits of the Russian empire on the banks of the Danube, the French Emperor showed a temporary disposition to desert his ally, which, if persisted in, would have rendered it a matter of doubt how far England could act with him for the future. The misunderstanding, however, speedily passed away. As a nation we were willing to leave the future to take care of itself, and to dwell with satisfaction on the better points in the character of our ally, which the war had served to elicit.

In the spring of 1855, while the Crimean war was still proceeding, the Emperor and his Empress paid a visit to England ; their progress through London was quite an ovation, the whole population having lined the streets from the Bricklayers' Arms Station in the extreme south-east to the Great Western Railway Station at Paddington, and welcoming them as they drove by in their carriage with the loudest and heartiest acclamations. It was observed, as the carriage drove up St. James's Street, that the Emperor pointed out to his fair wife the street (King Street) in which he had so long lived *en gan;on.* They *were* entertained for some days at Windsor Castle by the Queen, who either that year or the next returned the visit at Paris.

The same year is memorable as having witnessed the nations and crowned heads of Europe flocking to Paris, to take part in the inauguration of that great Industrial Exhibition which-ironical as the words must have sounded at the time-was intended to be the herald of peace and good will among men.

CHAPTER VIII.

THE ORSINI PLOT AND AUSTRIAN WAR.

EARLY in the year 1858, when the glories and disasters of the Crimean Campaign was still fresh in the memories of Englishmen, a diabolical, though happily unsuccessful, attempt was made on the Emperor's life by a miscreant named Orsini, who had abused the hospitality of England in order to concoct his plans, aided by a Dr. Bernard, a Frenchman resident, like himself, in London. In order to conciliate the wounded feelings of the Emperor, Lord Palmerston, who was at that time Prime Minister, brought into the House of Commons a Bill proposing certain alterations in the English law of conspiracy; but an outcry was raised against the measure, to the effect that it was undignified on the part of England to listen to French dictation, and popular feeling being roused to fever heat, the bill unfortunately was rejected. The failure of this measure surprised the Emperor not a little, and led to a feeling of irritation, which was increased by some absurd and bombastic speeches addressed to the Emperor by some of the colonels in the French army. A temporary suspension of cordial

relations between the French and English Govern·
ments followed ; but the Emperor did his best to
smooth the matter *over,* in which he was seconded
by the late Lord *Derby,* who had succeeded in the
interim to Lord Palmerston's Premiership. In spite
therefore of the acquittal of Dr. Bernard on his
trial at the Old Bailey on the 17th of April follow-
ing-an acquittal which all good and sensible citizens must now regret,-the good and friendly
relations which up to that time had existed between
the two Governments were happily re-established.
The Emperor knew the temper of the English
people and their Conservative instincts too well not
to perceive that no real sympathy was felt in England with the miscreants themselves, and he doubtless hoped that the law which seemed to harbour
such villains would be amended hereafter, when
the matter could be approached in a spirit of cool
deliberation.

In the course of this year (1858) was published
M. de la Guerronicre's pamphlet entitled "L'Empereur Napoleon III. et l'Angleterre," which created
a certain amount of interest in this country. It is
considered a calm and courteous investigation of
the relations which had for the previous six years
existed between Louis Napoleon and Great Britain,
and in it the reader is led to the conclusion that it
was the duty of our Government to take such measures as were consistent with constitutional principles to prevent conspiracies against the life of the
French Emperor. "As to the government of the

Emperor," says the author of the pamphlet in question, " it limits itself to explain the situation of affairs, to explain the causes of the irritation which the country manifested, and in other respects trusting to the loyalty of the English Government to give satisfaction to justice, to morality, to the interests of society, to international rights.

"We have explained our conduct with respect to England, we have shown what the Emperor Napoleon III. has been for her. vVc may boldly say that England has never found an ally more loyal, more persevering, and more independent of petty passions and rancour. That justice was rendered to him lately within the walls of the English Parliament, as it will be rendered to him by history; and we accept that homage for France and for her Sovereign 9-S an honour. Hence we have every confidence that the English people will not allow themselves to be led away in a manner, as difficult to explain as it is impossible to _excuse, and that their good sense, their patriotism, rising above false interpretations, the alliance of the two countries will stand the trial of these last incidents."

On the relations between France and Italy the Orsini conspiracy had a singular effect. The plotters arrested were Italians, and it was clear that Italian rather than French freedom was the object they expected to gain by the Emperor's death. The conspirators were condemned to death, and two suffered it. Many curious stories were circulated at the time, as to the foundation for which it would be rash to pass an opinion ; but from that time an impression, for which no one could give any tangible reason, began to pervade the public mind that Piedmont would once more renew her quarrel with Austria on behalf of the rest of Italy, and that this time she would not enter on war without allies. Piedmont was then under thesrule of Cavour, who had induced his sovereign to join the allies in the Crimean war, and thus entitled his country to have a voice in the general settlement of Europe. The wily Italian minister paid a visit to France and had several private interviews with the Emperor, the objects of which were afterwards sufficiently disclosed by events, though at the time it was studiously sought to divest these interviews of all political importance. Europe was repeatedly assured that France had no intention to go to war-nay, that she was incapable of war, for her army was wholly on a peace footing-a pretext which was more eagerly resorted to when it was proposed as a test of sincerity that there should be a general disarmament throughout Europe.

However, on New Year's Day, 1859, when, as usual, the representatives of foreign sovereigns repaired to the Tuileries to pay their formal visit to Emperor, the latter took occasion to explain to the Austrian minister that he felt that he had a just complaint against his master. Immediately it was assumed in every quarter of Europe that a war with Austria was at hand; and, in spite of the efforts of the other powers, including England, to

smooth   over the cause of irritation, the Austrian
Emperor resolved to invade Piedmont.   The word
of command was given ; an Austrian force appeared
in arms in the latter country.   Louis Napoleon led
an army to the aid of his allies, and the Austrians
were defeated at Magenta and Solferino, the French
Emperor commanding in person at the latter battle.
Soon afterwards, however, and somewhat unexpect-
edly, he offered terms of peace, which his Austrian
brother did not see it to be his interest to refuse,
and the brief war was concluded by what is known
as the Peace of Villafranca.   The terms, however,
were not such as were palatable   to the Italians,
who regarded them as a virtual abandonment of
their cause.   In consequence of this act both Lom-
bardy   and the Duchies were ceded to Victor
Emmanuel,   Venetia being left still subject to
Austria.

In the words of the writer already quoted, " at
the beginning of the war the Emperor had issued a
proclamation   that he had come to set Italy free
from the Alps to the Adriatic.   He laid down his
arms, however, when little more than the Duchy of
Milan was free from the grasp of the German. The
treaty of Villafranca did little more than ratify
that state of things.   Austria, that would hardly
recognise Piedmont through the negotiations, now
ceded Milan to France, and Louis Napoleon, in his
turn, made it over to Victor Emmanuel ; but the
rest of the peninsula was to remain under the sway
of its old rulers.   Napoleon, however, had evoked

a spirit of patriotism in the minds of the Italians, on which he had not calculated. His favourite idea was understood to be that the peninsula should be formed into a confederation of independent States, with the Pope at their head. Very different were the aspirations of the Italians themselves, with whom the unification of Italy had become a passion. One by one the inhabitants of the old duchies-of Tuscany, of Modena, and of the States of the Church-rose against their rulers, expelled them from their palaces, and by universal suffrage declared for a union with the kingdom of Piedmont. And last of all the expedition of Garibaldi revolutionised Naples and Sicily, and added these splendid possessions to the crown of Victor Emmanuel. There can be no doubt that these movements were secretly fomented and encouraged by the thoroughly Italianised wit of the Minister Cavour. The sequel is matter of history: Italy became a nation minus Venetia and Rome ; but the result was neither agreeable to the Emperor nor the French nation, who were the more annoyed, as they were after all the most responsible for the result. One material advantage the French empire gained from the war. Savoy and the whole French slope of the Alps became added to the French empire, and although such cession was very much against the views of the English and other European cabinets, the Emperor perseveringly held to his own views and prevailed,"

In the following year Louis Napoleon showed the weight of his influence on European politics by formally leading the way in acknowledging Victor Emmanuel as not only King of Sardinia, but King also of Italy.

CHAPTER IX.

MEXICO; DENMARK; ITALY. (1861-67.)

IT was in the year 1861, when at the zenith of his power as Emperor of France, and to a great extent the acknowledged arbiter of the destinies of Europe, that Louis Napoleon was led to give his sanction to an enterprise which he hoped would divert the minds of his people from home-politics, and afford a field in which ardent spirits might find military employment and-that end of a Frenchman's aspirations-glory. Accordingly, having obtained the concurrence of England and Spain, he organised an expedition against Mexico, with the avowed intention of demanding redress forcertain injuries inflicted, or, at all events, alleged to have been inflicted, on subjects of the respective countries, and for the payment of a debt which was obstinately resisted and repudiated by Mexico. As, however, it appeared to the English and Spanish Cabinets that the Emperor had other objects in view besides those which he publicly alleged, and that his ideas were rather too visionary for a practical people, Great Britain and Spain seceded from joint action with the French Emperor in April, 1862, leaving him to prosecute the war thenceforward alone.

Undaunted, notwithstanding, by this withdrawal, he persevered in the work which he had under· taken, and, after some battles in which many lives were sacrificed, he so far succeeded as to establish in that distant country an imperial form of government, the crown of which the Archduke Maximilian, brother of the Emperor of Austria, was induced to accept in October, 1863. In the following June, the new Emperor, accompanied by his young Empress, entered the capital; and imagining that the throne of his own creation was firmly established, Louis Napoleon entered into an agreement with the United States to withdraw his troops. This was accomplished' early in 1867, when the last detachments of the French army left the country. What followed is well known. The Em· peror, left to his own resources and unsupported by French bayonets, unable to defendhimself against a popular outbreak, was murdered in cold blood; and the neglect of the French Emperor to avenge the wrong became the first sign to the world of a loss of *prestige* which in the long run worked his ruin by unsettling and destroying the general belief in his all but omnipotence as an Emperor and a general. If it be true that "nothing succeeds like success," it is equally certain that nothing tends more to failure than the fact of having failed already. In the words of an able writer-e-

" That which was meant to be the crowning act, but which proved the great mistake, of Loui s Napoleon's life was the Mexican cxpedition- that dark and romantically tragic page of modern history. For the final catastrophe-the death of Maximilian-the Emperor was not answerable, as his troops offered to escort the unfortunate Prince and his friends out of the country, and it was only on his obstinately refusing to accept their offer that they were reluctantly constrained to abandon him to his fate ; but still the tragedy following so close upon the humiliation which the United States had inflicted upon him, was generally associated with the Emperor's name, and he was held answerable for every one of the consequences of the ill-starred expedition which he had planned."

For an account of the Emperor's policy in the eventful year of 1864, I must be indebted to the admirable life of the late Emperor, which was pub- lished in the *Standard,* of January roth :

"Great events were happening in Europe. The old quarrel between Germany and Denmark re- specting Schleswig-Holstein had broken out again; and a new insurrection in Poland, upheld for some time with great gallantry by the insurgents, but ultimately crushed with merciless severity by the Emperor of Russia, excited the sympathies of Europe. While these affairs were still imminent, the Emperor Napoleon had recourse to his favourite notion of a Congress of the European

States to settle the general affairs of Europe. The scheme was regarded with considerable jealousy by the other Powers, who suspected that the Emperor meant to make use of it as a means to obliterate the arrangements of the last Congress held in Europe-the Congress of Vienna. Still, none of the other States liked to take the initiative in refusing their assent, and answers in the affirmative, couched in various degrees of coldness, were received in Paris, till Earl Russell met the proposal by the point-blank query, what the Congress was intended to do. The Emperor was at the pains to enumerate four or five objects of European interest in which the Congress might be of use, on which our Minister, with merciless logic, proceeded to show that every one of these objects would be better arranged without a Congress than with one, and bluntly refused his assent. This was conclusive as to the fate of the Congress ; but it did not improve the friendly relations of the Emperor towards the English Ministry. Other causes increased his irritation. And the day speedily arrived when this alienation told with crushing effect. The Schleswig-Holstein question had culminated in the invasion of the country by an allied force of Austrians and Prussians. England, who had made herself peculiarly responsible for the integrity of Denmark, appealed to France and to Russia, joint parties to an old treaty in favour of Denmark, to avert the storm, but in vain. A conference was indeed held in London; but no solution

of the difficulty could be found, and England was
subjected to the mortification of seeing Schleswig·
Holstein torn from her ally without daring to lift a
hand in her defence, though just before, her Prime
Minister had declared in the face of the world that
if Austria and Prussia invaded Schleswig-Holstein,
they would find it was not the Danes only they had
to meet. Probably the humiliation -of England
was never so complete as at that moment, and the
revenge of Louis Napoleon on the English Ministers for a number of minor slights was never before
so ample. The tragedy of Mexico had not then
horrified Europe, and Napoleon still stood forth in
the zenith of his power: He made an effort to
improve his relations with Italy, which, in spite of
the great services he had rendered, had never been
very cordial. The great thorn in the side of the
Italians was the presence of the French garrison
at Rome, while the ayowed resolution of the
Italian people to make Rome their capital at the
first opportunity made his hold on that city only
the more tenacious. But now a compromise was
effected. Italy undertook to make Florence her
capital, thus practically, though not in name,
renouncing that dignity for Rome. France, on
her side, agreed to withdraw her garrison within
two years from the King taking up his abode irt
his new capital. Italy also promised that she
would not attack, nor suffer others on her territory
to attack, the Pope in his capital, while both parties
reserved to themselves liberty of action in case of

any insurrection within the Papal boundaries. This treaty, we may observe, was of short duration. It was kept indeed so far that Florence did become the Italian capital, and the French garrison did withdraw within the stipulated time, but on an insurrection taking place, fomented on the outside by Garibaldi, while both the French and the Italian Ministries showed considerable hesitation in the matter, the French garrison was restored and the insurrection was put down."

In order to fill up the historical interval between "the Schleswig-Holstein difficulty" and the great European war, which transferred the leadership of European politics from the Court of the Tuileries to that of Berlin, I am again compelled to acknowledge my obligations to a writer in the *Standard*, who thus epitomizes that eventful period :-

" The second great misfortune of the Emperor's life was now at hand. The Austrians and Prussians having entered into possession of Schleswig-Holstein fell to quarrelling over the spoil. Indeed, the union of the two Powers had never been cordially sincere. It was a rivalry for the headship of Germany, and Austria had entered into the war not that she cared for the matter, but that she would not abandon the lead of the minor states to Prussia. The quarrel widened every day, and while each protested its desire for peace each eagerly pressed on its preparations for war. Prussia made alliance with Italy, who was bribed to enter into hostilities with Austria by the prospect of obtaining Venetia.   There remained France to be considered.   Count Bismarck, the Prussian Minister, had sounded the Emperor upon that point.   What passed between them remains of course among the secrets of diplomacy, but it was generally believed that in that great crisis of Prussia's fate the Minister was not averse to purchasing the neutrality of Napoleon by some rectification of the French fron- tier at some other nation's expense, and that he was saved from coming to any direct bargain in the matter by the haughty and independent posi- tion assumed by the Emperor himself, who fancied that he could make better terms for himself by stepping in at the proper time between the con- tending combatants,   than   either   of them were singly likely to offer him.   His anticipation seemed to be that, after a long and sanguinary conflict, . both the parties would be so exhausted that they would be unable to prevent him from taking such a course as he might deem most expedient.   The calculation appeared   to be founded on the most assured conclusions, and yet it was utterly ,con- founded by the actual events.   The long and san- guinary conflict ,turned out to be a war of seven days, in which the Austrians were out-manceuvred , out - marched, out - generalled, and utterly over- thrown by their opponents.   In the first moments of their reverses the Austrians applied to the French Emperor at least to use his influence with the Italians to stop their hostilities, and they ceded Venetia to him as the price by which he might buy them off. The Emperor undertook the rmssion, and had the mortification to find that the Italians, creatures as they were of his own, disregarded alike his threats and his blandishments, and remained loyal to their engagement with the Prussians. Peace was made, but it was a peace in the adjustment of which the French Emperor was allowed to exercise the very slightest influence, and the issue of which was to make Prussia, the neighbour of France, her equal in the compactness of her dominions, and nearly her equal in numerical strength. The irritation, not only of the French Emperor, but of the whole French people, was extreme, and such as severely weakened the prestige of the second Empire, and prepared the way for the great events which followed."

CHAPTER X.

THE GERMAN WAR.

IN August, 1869, as all the world knows, the Centenary of the first Napoleon's birth was celebrated in France ; but, owing to continued indisposition, the Emperor himself was unable to take part in the rejoicings, and was obliged to send his little son, then just thirteen years old, to distribute the rewards to the troops. The newspapers at the time told us that the young Prince on this occasion acquitted himself well and successfully, that the soldiers themselves were well pleased with his "self-possession and his good seat in the saddle," and that he on his part, though, as yet, he had not received that " baptism of fire„ which came to him twelve months afterwards, was "well satisfied with the appearance of the troops under review." Alas ! how speedily and how painfully was his father about to be taught by experience, that there is nothing more deceitful than" appearances." At that moment, it is to be feared, while all was outwardly so fair to look upon, that the French army was wanting in accoutrements, wanting in means of transport, wanting in discipline, and wanting, above all, in that loyalty and personal attachment to its head, without which the best generalship must turn out a failure. The Empress, at the same time, as representing her husband, made a journey to the East, where she was present at the opening of the Suez Canal. In the course of her journey she paid a visit to Constantinople, and also to the Island of Corsica, in order to see the old home of the Bonapartes at an era so memorable in history as the Napoleonic centenary.

It is not a little strange that the cloud that heralded the great European war of 1870.71, a war which brought Germany and France face to face in a struggle for life or death, and in its issue changed not only the fortunes of Louis Napoleon, but the very map of Europe, should have arisen in a quarter so little to be expected beforehand as Spain. But so it was. The Spanish' insurrection of September, 1868, resulting in the dethronement of Queen Isabella, left the Crown of that country vacant, and after the lapse of more than a year it was offered to Prince Leopold of Hohenzollern Sigmaringen, a distant connection of King William of Prussia. There is no reason to suppose that the Prussian sovereign actively espoused his candidature, and when it was found that his acceptance of the Crown would cause jealousy and offence to French susceptibilities, he even dissuaded him frt>m going further in the matter. This, however, was not enough reparation for the Cabinet of the Tuileries, or rather for the French people, who, ever ready to take up arms, even though unprovoked, in the quest of military glory, almost with one voice, both in the Assembly and in the public press, required the Prussian King to disclaim all intention to interfere with respect to any future possible candidate. This insolence was too much for the Prussian monarch to swallow contentedly, and he declined to give any such promise. This refusal was declared by the people and the advisers of the Emperor to be a *casus bellz',* and accordingly they resolved that to war they would go. Louis Napoleon, who had but lately recovered from an illness, and had so lately let slip, or, at ~11 events, slackened the reigns of his own Imperial rule, found himself unable to resist or even to control the popular impulse, and allowed war to be declared in his name, though he must have had at the time his own strong suspicions that France was in no condition to go to war on a sudden with a power so well prepared at all points as Prussia. His own army, he had reason to fear, in spite of all the boastings and bravados of French citizens, was deficient in discipline, and had lost much of its ancient faith both in him and also in itself; and it must have been with many an anxious misgiving that he signed his name to the declaration of war which was drawn up by his ministers. However, the die was already cast ; he had virtually" crossed the Rubicon" when he transferred the supreme power from himself to his cabinet.   It was too late now to calculate chances.

It was indeed too late to recede;   in a few hours the fickle mob of Paris were crowding the Boulevards, echoing from lip to lip " a Berlin," and singing the Marseillaise;   even the Premier, M. Emile Ollivier, seemed to have lost his head in the whirl of excitement, and declared that the nation went to war "with a light heart."   Alas ! they and he little knew what six short weeks would bring forth.

War against Prussia was formally declared on the 15th of July; but, when every chance of success depended on immediate action, nearly a fortnight was wasted in making those preparations which the Emperor flattered himself had been made long before, and it was not until the 28th that he left St. Cloud for the seat of war on the borders of the Rhine.   He reached Metz that evening, and on the next day assumed nominally the chief command of the army.   I say nominally, because it is clear that from the first he allowed himself to be hampered by his generals, and the usual fate which attends divided counsels followed immediately.   On the second of August, a fortnight at least too late, offensive operations were commenced by the French, who, on that day, shelled and took the petty town of Saarbruck, where the Prince Imperial received what the Emperor seriously, but with bad taste, denominated "his Baptism of Fire."   This phrase occurred in a despatch from the Emperor to the Empress, of which the following is a translation:-

" Louis has been christened under fire. He was admirably cool, and not in any way excited. A division belonging to the army, under General Froissard, took possession of all the heights which overlook the left bank of Saarbruck. The Prussians made but a faint resistance. We were at the front, and the balls and bullets fell at our feet. Louis has kept one ball which fell close to him. Some of the soldiers actually cried at seeing him so calm. We lost only one officer and ten men killed."

French vanity was flattered for a moment, but for a moment only; for within the next four days the French troops had sustained severe losses and defeats at Weissenberg, Woerth, and Forbach.

The news was flashed to Paris by the telegraphic wires, and at first it was not believed ; but when a third defeat was announced, the excitement on the Boulevards knew no bounds. The generals were reproached with incapacity, cowardice, and treachery ; the Emperor, who the fickle mob had almost deified as he left the city for the seat of war ten days previously, was denounced as a miscreant and a traitor, and made the scapegoat, not of the Bonapartists only, but also of the army and the nation. It was the old story over again of the fall of Sejanus. Then, finally, when it became clear that the tables of war were turned, and that there was nothing to prevent the Prussians

from marching straight on Paris, the city itself was
declared, August zth, in a state of siege. Two
days later, M. Ollivier and his colleagues threw up
their posts and quitted Paris in order to save their
lives, and a temporary government, with Palikao
for its head, and under the Empress as Regent, was
devised, as the best possible expedient for the
moment. Marshal Bazaine was now made Com-
mander-in-Chief of the army ; the Emperor, having
resigned to him such nominal power as he held,
wandered hither and thither, almost maddened by
the disasters that had befallen his army, and which
he knew would be visited on his own devoted
head. For from the first, even before a shot was
fired, it was felt by him that on the issue of this
war depended all the hopes of his dynasty, and
that the war depended for its issue on two points,
good preparation and speedy action ; and now he
must have feared that both those points were lost,
past recall.

Meantime the disaster of Woerth was to pale
away before another and more important blow, by
the side of which the reverses sustained up to that
date were but as nothing. For, on Saturday, September rst, the whole French army, or rather armies,
were defeated in a most sanguinary encounter
at Sedan, in which it is clear from the testimony of eye-witnesses that the Emperor, sick and
suffering with an internal disease, showed the
valour of a hero, and made a desperate effort to
meet from Prussian bullets that death which at

all events would have then come at the happy
moment to his rescue, and saved him from the insults and gibes of his own craven-hearted countrymen, and possibly enshrouded his end in a halo of
something like glory.

But it was not to be so. Unfortunately he bore
about with him a " charmed life : " the bullets
whistled on every side around him, and shells ex-
ploded close beside him, but he was unwounded.
Then seeing, from a strategic point of view, not
only that all was lost, but that it was possible to
prolong the unequal strife only at a cost of
French blood which he rightly hesitated to shed
even in the cause of his throne and his dynasty, he
sent a white flag of truce to the Prussian King, and
offered at once to surrender his sword as a prisoner
of war. The King, in the presence of Count Bismarck, received his enemy's sword in token of formal
surrender, and the Empire and dynasty of Napoleon III. were at an end. It had fallen by a single
blow, and great was the fall of it.

And if now his sun went down in cloud and
storm, it was more owing to the force of circumstances than to any inherent defects in his own
discharge of his exalted office. Debarred by
physical weakness from holding the command of
the expeditionary army, limited by recent constitutional concessions in the government of home
affairs, and hampered by the prevalence of divided
counsels, he was prevented from bringing the
hitherto powerful aid of his great genius to bear

on the destinies of the country for which he lived,
and for whose regeneration he had done so much.
France was deprived of his rule just when she
wanted it most in the cabinet and in the field.
Let it never be forgotten, when the events of to-day
are remitted to the domain of history, that in this
heroic struggle with Prussia France fought not
with, but practically without, the Emperor Napoleon.   Had he retained the physical ability to lead
the army, as he had led it at Solferino and Magenta, the King of Prussia and the Crown Prince
might have found that they had a different host to
reckon with.   Had he, on the other hand, retained
the control of the administration at Paris; as once
he possessed it, he might have infused a spirit
throughout France which would have been equal
to the crisis; and the unfailing replenishment of
the troops would have sustained the defensive
power of the army, and have averted the hideous
catastrophes which, one after another, the superior
numbers of the German forces inflicted upon it.
But Napoleonic traditions required that the Emperor should take the field, while the new Constitution required that the cabinet should direct the
domestic policy.   Both were unequal to their
work : the Emperor from bodily weakness-the
cabinet from political incapacity.   France was thus
forsaken of her strength at both ends, while the
enemy, strong in numbers, admirable in generalship, and magnificently ministered to, strode on
from victory to victory against the flower and

chivalry of what, till then, was thought to be the greatest military Power in Europe.

In the words of a writer in a contemporary, " The supreme hour of ruin, dispersion, defeat, and surrender of the third of the great armies which have gone forth within one short month to face the invader has sounded; the 'bitter end' of that cruel war which the Emperor so proudly and hastily proclaimed, has come; the march to Berlin, which on the 25th of July was commenced amid the vociferous acclamations of the Parisian populace, has stopped short on the soil of France herself, and Napoleon, a well-guarded prisoner, is at this hour being transmitted by his conqueror through neutral Belgium, by Liege and Verviers, probably through Aix-Ia-Chapelle and the cis-Rhenane provinces of Prussia to Cologne, across Westphalia, and so to Cassel,* on the Fulda, where, at the Castle of Wilhelmshohe, the King of Prussia has appointed the residence of the dethroned ruler of France to live. Of this place, ninety miles north-east of Frankfort, we may note, that the Wilhelmshohe, which gives its name to a suburb, was a country seat of the Electors of Hesse-Cassel, and is ominously called, in the Prussian gazetteer, ' the German Versailles ! ' "

* The suburbs of Cassel are extremely beautiful, and abound in delightful promenades. That of Wilhelmshohe is especially rich in this respect, containing the Augarten (Meadow-garden), and the gardens which surround the Electoral Palace, which are famous for a fountain that sends a column of water 12 inches in diameter to a height of 200 feet. It is distant about 400 miles in a straight line from Paris, 100 from Cologne (the nearest point of the Rhine), and 300 from Lauterbrunn (the nearest point of French soil).

Early the following week, without further loss of time, the fallen Emperor was transported to the Chateau of Wilhelmshohe, where he was treated by his Conqueror with all the consideration due to fallen greatness.

In the meantime a series of terrible events had happened at Paris. For a time endeavour was made to conceal from the French nation the whole extent of the disaster ; but as soon as the intelligence of the loss of the flower of the French army and the surrender of the Emperor was sent on by. telegraph to the Empress and her ministers, the popular excitement was terrific. It is needless to add that the new administration were all deposed by violence, and that the reins of power were seized by a host of those worthless creatures who rise like scum to the surface, when the seething waters are troubled in the caldron. It is possible that Emile Ollivier and his colleagues were not the best or the ablest of advisers, and that Palikao was scarcely found equal to the crisis ; but these and such as these, were first-rate statesmen compared with the noisy and inexperienced rabble who rushed to the Tuileries, the Hotel de Ville, and the other public buildings, and seized promiscuously on the vacant portfolios, reviling their fallen chief as the " Man of Sedan ! "

And the brave and good Empress, what of her ? The story is short and plain, and will be fresh in the memories of most of my readers.

Her tale shall be told in the words of an eye·

witness in a letter dated from the Carlton Club, and published in the *Daily Telegraph* at the time :-

" Sir,-So far as I have been able to see, the accounts of the Empress's escape from the revolutionised capital on Sunday, which have been published in this country, are imperfect and inaccurate. I have just returned from Paris, where I had special opportunities of observing the stirring events of Sunday ; and I give you what I know to be the true story of her Majesty's escape. The deposition of the Napoleon dynasty was voted in the Corps Legislatif about one o'clock on Sunday afternoon. At two o'clock M. Pietri-then Prefect of Police-rushed breathlessly into the Empress's apartments at the Tuileries with the startling announcement and wanting :-' The *dlc/wance* has been declared. I have not a moment to lose. Save your life, Madame, as I am now hastening to save my own!' Then he disappeared-and with good reason, too, for the revolutionary Government would give something to be able to lay hands upon him now. The Empress found herself alone with her old and trusty secretary and friend, Madame le Breton, and with M. Ferdinand de Lesseps, who both earnestly urged her to fly at once. But her high spirit made this a most unpalatable 'counsel, 'It was a cowardice-une *laclt.ete-to* desert the palace. She would rather be treated as was Marie-Antoinette by the mob than seek safety in an unworthy flight.' For a time all persuasion was useless; but at length her Majesty's mood

calmed somewhat, and she saw the utter uselessness
of remaining. Attended   only by the two companions I have named, the Empress fled through
the long gallery of the Louvre ; but suddenly her
course was stopped short by a locked door. The
little party could distinctly hear the shouts of the
crowds who were invading the private gardens of
the Tuileries. M. de Lesseps, to gain time, proposed that he should go out on the terrace and get
the soldiers on guard to hold back the people for a
few minutes, while in addition he would delay the
crowds by addressing them. The [resort to this
expedient was not necessary. Madame le Breton
found the key, opened the door that had obstructed
their progress, and gave egress to her Majesty-
who, accompanied only by her tried friend, issued
into the street at the bottom of the Louvre. There
they hurriedly entered a common *fiacre,* not without risk of detection on the spot ; for a diminutive
gamin de Paris, not more than twelve years old,
shouted, "Voila l'Irnperatrice !' Luckily, no one
about heard or heeded him; and the cab got safely
away with the two ladies. Thus narrowly did she
escape with her life,-for there were not wanting
cowards in the surging crowd who cried *à la guillotine.*
They drove to M. de Lesseps's house in the Boulevard de Malesherbes, where the Empress sat until
she was joined by M. de Metternich, who did what
he could to facilitate her departure to a place of
safety. Later in the evening, the Empress, still
accompanied by Madame Le Breton, drove to the

Gare du Nord, escaped all detection-thanks to the thick veil which she wore-and at seven o'clock rolled safe and unsuspected away towards the coast of Trouville, spending the best part of three days on the way. But even here means had to be sought for reaching England. Fortunately for the fugitives, the *Gazelle* cutter lay in the harbour, and was to sail on the following day for England with Sir John and Lady Burgoyne. Lady Burgoyne had arrived on board that evening from Switzerland, but the yacht, with Sir John on board, had been lying some ten days in the harbour waiting Lady Burgoyne's arrival from Switzerland, which had necessarily been much delayed by the present state of things on the Continent. The first intimation Sir John Burgoyne received that other persons wished to cross to England in the *Gazelle* with Lady Burgoyne, was a few hours before the time appointed for the *Gazelle* to weigh her anchor, when the Empress presented herself, announced her rank and difficult position, and claimed his protection as an English gentleman. There had been no suspicion by Sir John Burgoyne of the Empress's presence or intended presence in the port. Under such unexpected conditions he acted as an Englishman would act. Lady Burgoyne was introduced to the Empress, who became her guest for the voyage across the Channel. It was not, however, before her time, which had been already fixed-viz., at seven o'clock on the succeeding morning, the 7th inst., that the *Gazelle* gave signs of leaving harbour for England, and then, with a large British ensign flying from her peak, she sailed leisurely out of the harbour, in charge of a French pilot. At 7.30 a.m. the pilot was discharged, and the *Gazelle* stood across the Channel for England. For thirty miles from the French land the little cutter had a fair wind, but then the wind suddenly chopped round to the N.W., and the remainder of the voyage was made under a three reefed mainsail, foresail, and storm jib in the teeth of a fresh gale. The *Gazelle's* seamen knew nothing of the Empress of the French being aboard, but they probably made shrewd guesses among themselves as to her rank. However that may have been, no man left the deck during the night's work across, and every one seemed anxious to shorten the distance between the two lands as much as possible. The *Gazelle* completed her voyage across the Channel by dropping anchor in Ryde Roads at 3.35 a.m on Thursday." After landing at Ryde from the *Gazelle,* the Empress crossed by steamer to Portsmouth, and proceeded to join the Prince Imperial at Hastings, where she fixed her head-quarters at an hotel until the following February, while the Emperor was still a prisoner at Wilhelrnshohe, when she entered upon the tenancy of Camden House, at Chislehurst, where her husband has just breathed his last. It may be interesting to know that this mansion, which now belongs to Mr. Strode, and though its memory is associated with a murder of its then occupants some sixty years since, was once the property of the antiquary William Camden, and afterwards Lord Chancellor Camden, who took his title from the place. It is a somewhat gloomy and old-fashioned residence, on the west side of Chislehurst-common, screened from the wind on all sides by trees, and from all intruders by high walls and old-fashioned iron-gates.

In the following month of March, having in the interim paid a flying visit to her husband at Wilhelmshohe, she welcomed him on his arrival in England by way of Ostend and Dover. Here the Imperial, or if I must be strictly accurate, the ex-Imperial family, have lived in quiet and retirement for nearly two years, their wish for privacy, on the whole, being more carefully observed than was possible in the gay towns of Hastings or St. Leonard's, The Empress, though often strongly solicited by adventurers, more or less selfishly interested in the game of chance, and anxious to use her as a pliant tool, has hitherto maintained the strictest silence and reserve as to the affairs of France, her husband, herself, and her son. At times she has been cruelly libelled,* and there have not been wanting those who accused her of having interfered in the fate, if not in the policy, of that distressed country, towards the shores of which she doubtless often strained her eyes, both at Hastings and at Chislehurst.

---

* For instance, in the month of August, 1i70, a libellous state•
blent on both the Empress of tl\e French and the Queen of England
appeared in the "Times," in the form of a telegram from its Berlin

During the last two years of his life, the Emperor, though he bore his past reverses with fortitude, looked feeble and bent in body, and a wreck of his former self. The only times on which he broke silence were in February, 1871, when he addresssd a proclamation to the French people, placing on record the causes of his defeat, and in the summer of 1872, when he issued, or rather allowed to be issued in his name, a pamphlet on the same subject. The following is the text of his Majesty's Proclamation :-

CASSEL, *Feb.* 8.

" Betrayed by fortune, I have preserved since my captivity that profound silence which is misfortune's mourning. So long as the Armies of France and Germany confronted one another I abstained from · all steps or words which might have divided the public mind. I can no longer be silent in face of the disasters of my country without appearing to be insensible to its sufferings. When I was compelled to surrender myself a prisoner I could not treat for Peace ; my decisions would have seemed dictated by personal considerations ; I left

correspondent, which was to the effect that the Queen had written, "In reply to the Empress Eugenie's letter about a week ago, regretting her inability to mediate ; " and that her Majesty had " observed that in Constitutional England mediation must proceed from the Cabinet, but that the Cabinet did not think the time come." The letter to which this reply had been invented was never received by the Queen, and was never written by the Empress. In the case of the Empress Eugenie, the story was a cruel calumny, which, if believed in Paris, might have led to consequences too horrible to contemplate.

to the Governmentof the Regent the duty of de-
ciding whether the interests of the nation required
a continuance of the struggle. Notwithstanding
unheard-ofreverses,France was not subdued. Our
strongholds still held out, few Departments were
invaded, Paris was in a state of defence,and the
area of our misfortunesmight have been limited.

"But while attention was fixed upon the enemy
an insurrectionbroke out in Paris. The seat of the
National Representatives was violated, the safety
of the Empress was threatened, a Governmentin-
stalled itself by surprise in the Hotel de Ville, and
the Empire, which the whole nation had just ac-
claimedfor the third time, was overthrown,aban-
doned by thosewho should have been its defenders,
Setting aside for a time my presentiments,I ex-
claimed,' What matter the dynasty if the country
can be saved!' and, instead of protestingagainst
the violencedoneagainst right, I desiredthe success
of the National Defence,and I have admired the
patriotic devotion shown by the offspring of all
classesand of all parties.

"Now that the struggle is suspended, that the
Capital, notwithstanding an heroic resistance,has
succumbed,and that all reasonablechance of vie·
tory has disappeared,it is time to ask for an account from those who have usurped powerof the
blood shed without necessity,the ruin heaped up
without reason,the resourcesof the country squan-
dered without control. ·

" The destinies of France cannot be abandoned

to a Government without a commission, which, while disorganizing the administration, has not left standing a single authority emanating from universal suffrage. The nation cannot long obey those who have no right to command. Order, confidence; and solid Peace will not be restored till the people has been consulted as to which is the Government most capable of repairing the national disasters.

" In the solemn circumstances in which we are situated, in the face of an invasion, and' with Europe attentive, it is important that France should be one in her aims and her desires as well as in her decisions. Such is the object towards which the efforts of all good citizens should tend.

"As regards myself, bruised by so much injustice and such bitter deception, I do not come for· ward to-day to claim rights which four times in 20 years you freely confirmed. In the presence of the calamities which afflict us there is no room for personal ambition. But so long as the people regularly assembled in its *comitia* shall not have manifested its will, it will be my duty to address myself to the nation as its real representative, and to tell it that all that may be done without your direct participation is illegitimate. There is but one Government which has issued from the national sovereignty, and which, rising above the selfishness of parties, has the strength to heal your wounds, to reopen your hearts to hope, and your profaned churches to *yout* prayers, and to bring back industry, concord, and peace to the bosom of the country."

The pamphlet already mentioned, and entitled "Campagne de 1870: Des Causes qui ont amene la Capitulation de Sedan ; par un Officier attache a l'Etat Major..General. Bruxelles, 1870," is a dis· claimer of the policy that culminated at the disaster of Sedan.

Before the war began, the Emperor knew it would be surrounded by great difficulties, and would not be a mere military promenade. He knew that Prussia was ready to call out, in a short time, ~,ooo men, and with the aid of the Southern States of Germany, could count upon 1,100,000 soldiers. France was only able to muster 6oo,ooo; and as the number of fighting men is never more than one-half the actual force, Germany was in a position to bring into the field 5 50,000 men, while France had only about 300,000 to confront the enemy. To compensate for this numerical inferiority, it was necessary, by a rapid movement, to cross the Rhine, separate Southern Germany from the North German Confederation, and by the *lclat* of a first success, secure the alliance of Austria and Italy. If the French were thus able to prevent the armies of Southern Germany from forming their junctions with those of the north, the effective strength of the Prussians would be reduced 200,000 men ; and the disproportion between the number of com- " batants thus much diminished. If Austria and Italy made common cause with France, then the superiority of numbers would, be in our favour. The Emperor's plan of campaign-which he con·

fided, at Paris, to Marshals MacMahon and Leboeuf alone-was to mass 1 50,000 men at Metz, 100,000 at Strasburg, and 50,000 at the Camp of Chalons, As soon as the troops should have been concentrated at the points indicated, it was the Emperor's purpose to immediately unite the two armies of Metz and Strasburg; and, at the head of 250,000 men, to cross the Rhine to Maxau, leaving at his right the fortress of Rastadt, and at his left, that of Germersheim. Meanwhile the 50,000 men at Chalons, under the command of Marshal Canrobert, were to proceed to Metz to protect the rear of the army and guard the north-eastern frontier. At the same time the fleet cruising in the Baltic would have held stationary in the north of Prussia, a part of the enemy's forces, obliged to defend the coast threatened with invasion. The sole chance, however, of this plan succeeding was to surpass the enemy in rapidity of movement, and here it was that it broke down. The organization of the army was unfortunately defective ; the Opposition having thwarted the Emperor's scheme of reforms, the troops comprising the army were dispersed over the whole country, the *materiel* was likewise scattered, and the generals were fettered by their limited powers and the red-tape stringency of the War-office. The Army of Metz, instead of 150,000 men, only mustered 100,000; that of Strasburg only 40,000 instead of 100,000; whilst the corps of Marshal Canrobert had still one division at Paris and another at Soissons; his artillery, as well as his cavalry, was not ready. Further, no army corps was even yet completely furnished with the equipments necessary for taking the field. The Emperor gave precise orders to the effect that the arrival of the missing regiments should be pushed on ; but he was obeyed slowly, excuse being made that it was impossible to leave Algeria, Paris, and Lyons without garrisons. It was under these circumstances, by the bold initiative of the German troops, who poured in simultaneously by the Sarre and by the Rhine, that the French were caught in the very act of formation. The Emperor would at once have fallen back upon Chalons, but was prevented by the Ministry at Paris, who urged that the abandonment of Lorraine could only produce a deplorable effect on the public mind. The effective force of the Army of Metz was brought up to 140,000 by the arrival of Marshal Canrobert with two divisions and the reserve, and it received orders for its concentration around Metz, in the hope that it might be able to fall upon one of the Prussian armies before they had effected their junction. Unfortunately, as if in this campaign all the elements of success were to be wanting, not only was the concentration of the army retarded *by* the combat at Spicheren and *by* the bad weather, but its action was paralysed by the absolute ignorance in which its leaders remained concerning the position and strength of the hostile armies. On the 14th of August, as also on the 16th, no one imagined that the whole Prussian army had to be dealt with; no one doubted at Gravelotte that Verdun could easily be reached on the morrow. At Paris they were no better informed. The Emperor decided to give the command to Marshal Bazaine, and to resume the conduct of the affairs of the country. The uninterrupted succession of disasters which followed produced in Paris a strong impression, and the Ministers, uneasy at this state of affairs, convoked the Chambers, without even a reference to the Emperor ; and from the time of their assembly it was, as it always is in public calamities, the Opposition which saw its influence increase, and which paralysed the patriotism of the majority and the progress of the Government. From this period Ministers appeared afraid to pronounce the name of the. Emperor ; and he, who had quitted the army, and had only relinquished the command in order to resume the reins of government, soon discovered that it would be impossible for him to play out the part which belonged to him. A dispute then arose between the Emperor and MacMahon on the one hand and the Ministry in Paris on the other, as to the next course to be pursued. The former were for falling back on Paris, the latter insisted on the relief of Bazaine, and finally carried their point. The delay at Rethel which retarded Marshal Mac-Mahon's march was due to commissariat difficulties. The intention of the Marshal was to reach Stenay, and from thence Montmedy, But the enemy was already in strength in the first of these two towns. Th~ Prussian army had made forced marches, while the French, encumbered with baggage, had occupied six days with fatigued troops in marching twenty-five leagues. It was, in fact, a race between the armies. The French lost, and their being shut in Sedan was the result. Such, as the Emperor remarks, was the consequence of a plan of a campaign imposed from Paris, and contrary to the most elementary principles of war. The Emperor confirms the statement that in his interview with the King of Prussia he attributed the war to a violent excitement of the public mind which he could not resist; and draws the following characteristic moral from the story :-" The successes of Prussia are due to the superiority of numbers; to the rigorous discipline of her army ; and to the empire exercised throughout Germany by the principle of authority. May our unhappy fellow-countrymen who are prisoners at least profit, during their sojourn in Prussia, by appreciating that which gives strength to a country-' the powers that be' respected, the law obeyed, the military and patriotic spirit dominating all interests and all op.nions ! . . . . To sum up, the army always reflects the state of society in which it has been formed. So long as authority in France was strong and respected, the constitution of the army presented a remarkable solidity ; but when the excesses of the tribune and of the press were permitted to enfeeble authority, and to introduce everywhere a spirit of criticism and insubordination, the army felt the effects of it fatally."

Words more quiet, more dignified, more truthful, were never spoken ; and it is the belief of all sound-judging persons, both here and abroad, that they will be shown to be true to the letter, by the mere lapse of time, that great touchstone which brings all things, sooner or later, to the test. For, as Sophocles tells us-

> "Time only doth a just man-show as just;
> But villains e'en in one brief day we know."

To the bar of future history, it is my firm belief that Louis Napoleon can appeal with confidence, and at that bar he will be judged, when the vile scum of the French Commune, and the gibes of ribald writers and pamphleteers who have cursed him as " The Man of Sedan " are buried in oblivion.

CHAPTER XI.

LAST ILLNESS AND DEATH.

I PURPOSELY draw a veil over the history of France and of Paris during the two years and a quarter which have elapsed since the fall of the Empire at Sedan. The Emperor of course knew that it would be madness, in the then temper of its fickle population, even to attempt to return, unless crowned with the laurels of a conqueror; and the brave Empress-Regent, happy in being able to effect her escape to England, has kept a discreet silence, both on personal and political questions, since she set her foot upon our shores. He and she fortunately were spared the sight of the destruction of the fair Palace of St. Cloud by Parisian shells, in the presence of the German enemy, who would have saved its *salons,* if possible; they did not see the Prussian King fixed in the proud palace of Louis XIV. at Versailles as his winter quarters, and the still sadder scene of French citizens firing their own " Hotel de Ville," as well as the regal and Imperial Tuileries, with matricidal hands. They were spared, too, the sight of an unoffending arch-

bishop, and priests, and nuns, and laymen per-
fidiously and cruelly massacred as " hostages," for-
sooth ! They saw, indeed, men like the *soi-disant*
Due de Rousillon, *r*with other equally distinguished
Frenchmen, skulking about in the back streets of
London,-forgetful of the old definition of a Duke,
*"Dux est qui ducit exerci!tmt,"*when- they ought
to have been placing their swords, like brave men,
at the disposal either of the Emperor, or of the
Republic of M. Thiers ; but a merciful Providence
saved the Imperial pair from witnessing the utter
demoralization, the overthrow, and destruction of
the fair city which Louis Napoleon and his employes
had done so much to beautify and enrich. Refusing,
also, to acknowledge in any way the acts of those
who since have swayed the destinies of France,
they earned the respect and regard of all enlightened
Englishmen by their dignified silence and neutrality.

There can be no doubt, both on other grounds
and also from the *posMnortem* examination of the
body, that although the Emperor's last sickness
was but of brief duration, he had suffered severely
in health for many years, though, from the constant
reticence and self-restraint which he practised, the
secret of his physical sufferings was known to few
save the Empress, and his faithful medical attendant,
Dr. Conneau. It will be remembered that as far
back as the August of 1869, he was unable through
bodily illness to be present with the army at the
Camp of Chalons on the centenary anniversary of
his uncle's birth, and that the Prince Imperial

represented him on that occasion, the Empress being on her way to Corsica, *en route* for Constantinople and the Isthmus of Suez. It will not be forgotten, too, how that he sat in the saddle for five hours at Sedan, suffering all the time excruciating agonies from the disease which was slowly and surely sapping his life. And when he landed in England, not quite two years ago, he was apparently weak and feeble, and stooped in gait, and presented, in fact, a marked contrast in the eyes of those who had known him in former times, The fact was, that even then the formation of stone in the bladder had commenced to create an irritation, which ultimately developed into actual and chronic disease.

Still he was able to take his customary walking exercise on Chislehurst Common almost to the end of last year, several of the early months of which he spent in the West of England, visiting Bath, Exeter, and Torquay, where he met once more his old but since departed friend, Sir John Bow. ring. Later in the summer he attended the meeting of the British Association at Brighton, and went thence to Cowes, returning to Chislehurst in September.

In July last, though conscious from surgical report that his condition was not satisfactory, the Emperor was urged to have a special examination of his condition made ; but he declined, though, after his return to Chislehurst, so rapid was the increase of the malady, that his Majesty was at

length forced, as it were, to submit. Upon the
report of Sir Henry Thompson, the eminent litho-
tritist, that a vesical calculus of phosphate character
of large size existed within him, the Emperor, on
the znd of January-just a week previous to his
death-" placed himself unreservedly in the hands
of his medical advisers, his only request being, that
whatever was to be done should be done quickly."
The operation of lithotrity was performed by Sir
Henry Thompson, "in the presence of Sir William
Gull and the Emperor's regular medical attendants,
Dr. Conneau and the Baron Corvisart. A second
operation was undergone on the following Monday,
when, as in the previous instance, a large quantity
of the calculus was crushed, which it was hoped
would be eventually carried off by the natural
action of the body. From this time the pain is
reported to have somewhat abated, and all apparently was going on well till the morning of
the following Thursday. On that day a third
operation was to have been performed at noon, the
doctors in attendance had during the preceding
night paid the strictest attention to their illustrious
patient, relieving each other by turns by the Emperor's bedside. Sir Henry Thompson, as an extra
precaution for the delicate operation he was to

---

* It is to be remarked that, in spite of the acknowledged celebrity
of more than one foreign surgeon, it was to an *Enclisk* surgeon that
the difficult and responsible duty of performing the operation,
under the effects of which he sunk, was entrusted by Louis Napo·
leon and his family,

perform, paid a visit to the Emperor at twenty-five minutes past ten, when, greatly to his surprise, after the cheeringsigns of little more than half-an. hour before, he observed a sudden change in the conditionofthe patient. Instantly the other medical attendants were summoned to the room, and it became at once apparent to all present that the Emperor was fast sinking. A carriage was despatched with all speed to Woolwich-some six miles distant-to fetch the Prince Imperial; but he arrived too late, as did all those other friends of the Emperor within reasonable distance to whom telegraphic messages had been sent instantly on the occurrence of the fatal change. The Empress had been immediately summoned, and arrived in a few minutes, not too late to be recognised, although the Emperor is said to have been too exhausted to speak distinctly. The last sign of consciousness the Emperor gave was a smile when the Empress kissed him. In the meantime Father Goddard, the Priest of Chislehurst, had been summoned in all haste; and he arrived in time to administer, not indeed the "Viaticum," but the Sacrament of Extreme Unction, and to read the prayers for a departing soul. A few minutes later, and all was over. Peacefully, without any convulsionor any expressionof suffering, his soul had passed away. So sudden had been the shock to the Empress, that she swoonedaway, and had to be removedin a state of insensibilityfrom the apartment.

Finem animse quee res humanas miscuit olim
Non gladii, non saxa dabunt, non tela, sed ille,

   *   *   *   *   *   *

Calculus.

"1-te is dead," writes the *Daily Te!egraplz,* "and of him we may say, as Bacon said of himself, 'his memory must be left to foreign nations, and "after a little while" to his own countrymen.' The day may come when another funeral train may pass through the Arc de Triomphe, when another Bonaparte may be laid beneath the shining cupola of Les Invalides ; when even the dreary crypt of the Capuchin Convent at Vienna may give up its dead, and the Due de Reichstadt shall sleep by the side of his father and cousin. Time is a healer as well as an avenger. For the nonce a quiet and obscure tomb may well suffice to receive him on whose character for evil or for good an impartial posterity has not yet had time to pronounce. It is enough to know that he died in honour and competence, at peace with all mankind, even his enemies; his eyes gazing at the Cross, and the kisses of his brave wife upon his brow."

Immediately after the death o(the Emperor, telegrams containing full details as to the actual cause of his decease, his final moments, and the condition of the Empress, were forwarded to Her Majesty the Queen, the Prince and Princess of Wales, and other members of the Royal Family, and to the crowned heads of Europe ; and, in reply, messages of condolence and sympathy were at once trartsmitted to the Empress in her great sorrow.

A *post-mortem* examination of the body was made next day by Dr. Burdon Sanderson. The following is a copy of the official report :-

" The most important result of the examination was, that the kidneys were found to be involved in the inflammatory effects produced by the irritation of the vesical calculus (which must have been in the bladder several years) to a degree which was not suspected, and if it had been suspected could not have been ascertained.

"The disease of the kidneys was of two kinds : there was, on the one hand, dilatation of both ureters and of the pelvis of both kidneys. On the left side the dilatation was excessive, and had given rise to atrophy of the glandular substance of the organ. On the other there was sub-acute inflammation of the uriniferous tubes, which was of more recent origin.

" The parts in the neighbourhood of the bladder were in a healthy state ; the mucous membrane of the bladder and prostatic urethra exhibited the signs of sub-acute inflammation, but not the slightest indication of injury. In the interior of the bladder a part of a calculus was found, the form of which indicated that half had been removed. There were besides two or three extremely small fragments, ·none of them larger than a hemp seed. The half calculus weighed about three-quarters of an ounce, and measured 1 inch by 1 5-16 inch. There was no disease of the heart nor of any other organ excepting of the kidneys. The brain and its membranes were in a perfectly healthy state. The blood was generally liquid, containing only a few small clots. No trace of obstruction by coagula could be found either ·in the venous system, in the heart, or in the pulmonary artery. Death took place by failure of the circulation, and was· attributable to the general constitutional state of the patient. The disease of the kidneys, of which this state was the expression, was of such a nature and so advanced that it would in any case have shortly determined a fatal result.

> (Signed) "J. BURDON SANDERSON, M.D.
> "Dr. CONNEAU.
> "Dr. Le Baron CoRVISART.
> "HENRY THOMPSON.
> "J. T. CLOVER.
> "JOHN FOSTER.

" CAMDEN PLACE, CHISLEHURST, *Jan.* 10."

Sir William Gull did not remain till the discussion that ensued on the completion of the autopsy ; and although not actually signing the report, he has, however, recorded his assent on all points but one, namely, the date of the origin of the calculus.

On the Sunday following the Emperor's decease, at St. Paul's Cathedral and Westminster Abbey, the Rev. William Rogers and Archdeacon Jennings, spoke of him at considerable length ; the former remarking, among other things, that instead of the mutual hatred between France and England for which we were once renowned, and which was proclaimed to be national, handed down as a heirloom from father to son, the late Emperor had taught both nations to become more united, and to live together as brethren, members of one family; whilst Archdeacon Jennings remarked that in the Emperor Napoleon we had a striking instance and an instructive example of the vicissitude of human fortunes and earthly greatness.

On this day the body of the Emperor underwent the process of embalming. It was afterwards re·moved to the principal *salon* or hall of the house, and on Tuesday the public were permitted to view him as he lay in state. The remains were placed immediately under the hall skylight, the light from which had been darkened by the tricolour standard of the legions which once were his. A small mortuary chamber, curtained off with black cloth, and escutcheoned with silver crowns and arms, hung from the ceiling to the floor; and in the centre of this enclosed space, which was lighted by candles, the coffin rested on an inclined plane, so that the face might be easily seen. A velvet pall, bearing the Imperial crown and " N," hung from the edges of the coffin to the floor, and the body was covered to the waist by the Emperor's cloak, thrown across the coffin. The body, with the hands clasped in the attitude of prayer, was clothed in the dress of a general of

K

division of the army of France-the same, it is
stated, which was worn by him at his memorable
interview with the Emperor of Germany after the
defeat at Sedan, and for the last time on his arrival
in captivity at Wilhelmshohe. Among those who
came specially to witness the lying-in-state were
the Prince of Wales, accompanied by his brother,
the Duke of Edinburgh, and Prince· Christian.
During the four hours in which the public-in
batches of 200 at a time, and all clothed in mourn-
ing-the familiar features of the late Emperor,
almost unchanged in appearance, though the eyes
were closed in death, were gazed upon for the last
time by the thousands of persons who were fortu-
nate enough to gain admittance.

Under the fine sky of a warm but dull January
morning, the funeral took place on the Wed-
nesday following the Emperor's death, in the
small church of St. Mary, at Chislehurst. The
distance from Camden Place to the sacred edifice
being only a few hundred yards, the procession
following the hearse was entirely on foot. The
religious service was performed by the Bishop of
Southwark, and the procession was headed by
twenty-five French workmen, in their rough daily
dress and blouse, one of whom carried the tri-
color. About eleven o'clock the hearse, drawn by
eight horses, caparisoned in velvet and escutcheoned trappings, left the house. The body of the
Emperor, was enclosed in three coffins, of which the
outermost was covered with purple velvet, studded

with nails, and ornamented with a Latin cross, and with the Imperial crown and initials, all in silver. A silver plate upon the coffin bore the following inscription :-

Napoleon III.,
Empereur des Francais.
Né a Paris
le 20 Avril, 1808;
Mort à Camden Place,
Chislehurst,
le 9 Janvier, 1873.
R. I. P.

Immediately following the hearse, as chief mourner, walked the Prince Imperial, in plain mourning clothes, and wearing the grand cordon of the Legion of Honour. Next came the representatives of the House of Bonaparte, in the order of their precedence, namely, Prince Napoleon, Prince Lucien Bonaparte, Prince Charles Bonaparte, and the Princes Charles and Joachim Murat. The rest of the procession was formed of the many distinguished and devoted Bonapartists who had come to this country for the purpose of paying their last tribute of respect to their late master. Among these were M. Rouher, one of the most trusted and able of the Imperial statesmen ; the Marquis de Lavalette, the last of the ambassadors to the Court of St. James's under the rule of the Empire; M. Pietri, the late Emperor's Prefect of Police; Vicomte Aguado, the Comte de Clary, General Fleury, and others, now or formerly of the Imperial Household ; Marshals Canrobert and Lebeeuf; Dr. Corvisart, who for years past had been one of the Emperor's personal physicians; and Dr. Conneau, the oldest servant of all, who thus ended forty years of close, faithful, and affectionate intercourse with his master, both in prosperity and adversity.

No member of the royal family of England was actually present at the funeral ceremony, but in accordance with the precedent of the funeral of Louis Philippe in 1850, Lord Sydney had a place of honour assigned to him in the procession as representing Her Majesty the Queen, whilst the Prince of Wales was represented by Lord Sheffield. The Lord Mayor of London also was present as representing the entire people of that nation whom the first Napoleon so wittily styled a "nation of shopkeepers."

On the conclusion of the religious service in the chapel, the body was deposited in its temporary resting-place in a small mortuary chapel on the southern side of the building.

So rests for the present, in a humble Kentish village, the once powerful Emperor and arbiter of the destinies of Europe-like Louis Philippe, his predecessor=-awaiting the day when, the wheel of fortune having changed, and the animosity of the present hour being forgotten, his ashes may be transferred to the land of his sires. Better that he should rest here among strangers, who are kindly friends of his widow and his son, than that he should be consigned to the Chapel of Les Invalides, where the first outbreak of popular frenzy might witness the violation of the sanctity of the tomb ! Yes ! as we look back on his career we are reluctantly obliged to own with the heathen poet:-

" Mors sola fatetur
Quantula sunt hominum corpuscula. „

The pretty village of Chislehurst, adjoining Bromley, in Kent, although scarcely more than a dozen miles from London, was well suited, by its re-tired position, to become the scene where Napoleon should close his earthly career. The house known as Camden Place,which was taken as a residence for the Empress Eugenie and the young Prince Imperial, shortly after their arrival in England, and where they were afterwards joined by the Emperor him-self, is an old-fashioned mansion in a small park adjoining the west side of the common at Chisle-hurst. It received its name (says Mr. Britton) in his " Beauties of England and Wales," from the famous antiquary and historian William Camden, who is said to have composed his" Annals of the Reign of Queen Elizabeth" during his latter years while resident on this estate. He was some time head master of Westminster School, and in 1597 was created Clarencieux King-at-Arms. He died at Camden Place in the month of November, 1623, and his body being removed to his residence in London, was carried thence to his last resting-place in Westminster Abbey in great pomp, the whole College of Heralds, in their official costume, as well as numbers of the nobility and persons of distinc-

tion joining in the procession. The estate of Cam·
den Place having passed by sale to several different
owners, came at length into the possession of Sir
Charles Pratt, Lord Chief Justice of the Court of
Common Pleas, who was raised to the peerage in
the year 1765 as Baron Camden, of Camden Place,
Kent. The populous London suburb of Camden
Town, which occupies a large part of the parish of
St. Pancras, along the Hampstead Road, derives
its name from the estate of this wealthy peer.   In
the park attached to Camden Place, Chislehurst, may
be seen that celebrated piece of architecture which
is commonly called " The Lantern of Demosthenes,
or Choragic Monument of Lysicrates,"   Camden
Place, we may add, now the property of a non-
resident owner, Mr. N. Strode, has a somewhat
sinister reputation in the neighbourhood, as the
scene of a brutal murder, just sixty years ago, for
which the murderer was executed at Maidstone.
The mansion is a comfortable country house,
not very large, built in light and dark brick.   The
front view is not in the least imposing, though the
details of the building, made irregular by various
projections surmounted with balustraded parapets,
harmonize well together.   A short drive leads
through trees and shrubberies to a gravel sweep
before the hall door, the hall itself forming a good
sized square, and being lighted by a skylight from
the roof. To the right and left of the hall are the
dining and drawing rooms, and on the side towards
the dining-room a rather fine staircase, the wall of

which is hung with large pictures, leads to a gallery from which branch the various doorways and passages of the upper story. The room in which the Emperor died is very small, and one chosen by himself as his own bed-chamber when he came first to reside at Camden Place.

The ashes of the Bonapartes, it has been remembered, have undergone almost as many vicissitudes as the members of that house have suffered in life, As Mrs. Hemans sings,-

> "Their graves are sever'd far and wide
> By mountain, stream, and sea."

Though it had always been the design of the great Napoleon that he should rest in a splendid vault in the Cathedral of St. Denis, where the Carlovingian and Merovingian Kings of France, and the Capets of the Bourbons are interred, he lies in the Chapel of the Hospital of Les Invalides at Paris. His son, the " King of Rome" is buried at Schonbrunn, his wife Josephine, at Malmaison, and his brothers in various places. It was at one time the intention of Louis Napoleon to lie in St. Denis, but he was deterred, it is said, by an omen, the fall of a stone upon the masons at their work. Accordingly, in the later years of his life, it is no secret that he made up his mind to establish the burial place of his dynasty at St. Leu, a village about six miles north of Paris, which, as I have said, gave a title to his parents, and where his father, his mother, his grandfather, and his elder brother, all repose. Accordingly, the ex-Emperor a few years since, changed the name of the village to Napoleon St. Leu; rebuilt and enlarged the church at great expense, and had constructed a special vault in the chancel, which was handselled by the removal into it of the coffins containing the remains of the four members of the family who were already in occupation. He issued, too, in his turn, a decree that this vault was thenceforth to be regarded as the burial place of the dynasty. The pillars, roof, and walls of the church are studded thickly with Imperial insignia, and in the recess behind the altar is an imposing monument of white marble, surmounted by a painting of St. Napoleon on a cloud. The monument is crowned by a life statue of ex-King Louis, and below, in parallel niches, are the busts of the other three occupants of the vault, with a brief biographical inscription in gold letters below. There can be no doubt that the remains of the late Emperor will ultimately be placed in the vault of the church of Napoleon St. Leu, in the place of sepulture which he himself chose and erected.

At the end of the ceremony, the Prince Imperial was greeted by the adherents of the Second Empire as Napoleon IV., and in that capacity at once held his first, though somewhat informal, *levee,* in the house where his father had died.

CHAPTER XII.

LOUIS NAPOLEON, AS STATESMi\N, AUTHOR, AND " THE ELDEST SON OF THE CHURCH."

AND now, having told the story of the late Emperor's life, from his birth at the Tuileries down to his death at Chislehurst, it is obviously my duty to add some brief reflections on his character, viewed in several lights.

First, then, as a statesman. In this *role,* I have already shown that in my own humble opinion, whatever may have been his faults and his failings, and however wanting his career was in final success, he was a wise and beneficent ruler, and indeed the best possible ruler for his native country, since that fair land has disowned and dethroned the white lily of the Bourbons which waved for a thousand years over the crown of France. He became a deep student of political economy and political science in early manhood, and the lessons which he then had leisure to learn, both in England and in Switzerland, he had the opportunity in later years to put to the test of experience. There can be no doubt that for nearly twenty years these were

crowned by that success which is so much adored
by the multitude; and that if an end had been put
to his career by a stray bullet at Solferino, his own
people, who now curse him as " the Man of Sedan,"
would have worshipped him as a demi-god.   Nay,
even had he fell, as he desired to fall, at Sedan, it
is quite. possible that they might have ascribed the
disasters of that day to the divisions existing between his generals, and that the chivalrous feeling
of France-if such an element be left in her-would
have rallied round a widowed Empress Regent and
her orphan boy.   Providence willed it otherwise,
and, like Hannibal and Pompey and Marius of old,
Louis Napoleon was not lucky in the moment of
his death.

I have spoken of him as a wise and prudent
ruler: in support of my assertion I could point to
the fact that years ago, in the terse and elegant
words of the *Times,* among " a nation of Protection-
ists he stood forth alone a freetrader," and that in
all the commercial arrangements   of France with
England he insisted on the great advantage to his
own country of free exports and imports.   In these
matters he was wont to take counsel, not only with
the diplomatic representatives of the English Court
and Cabinet, who probably knew very little of such
unimportant details,-but   with that old and expe-
rienced free-trader, the great friend of his middle
age, the late Sir John Bowring, whom he constantly
took into his counsels in private as well as in public
audiences.   It was at one such interview at the

Palace of St. Cloud-I believe, in the winter of 1860-that in the course of a lengthened and very intimate conversation with respect to the free interchange of national' commodities, that the Emperor, who was clothed in warm and comfortable winter garments, rubbed his trousers with both his hands, and said to his guest, "Why, *mon. ami,* Sir John, should not all my poor people here be enabled to purchase such materials of clothing as this, and give to you in exchange something that our country produces and yours does not?" It may be added here that the erection of a statue to Richard Cobden's memory in London, was largely due to the late Emperor's activity and energy.

I have stated repeatedly in the previous pages that the late Emperor was in reality on conviction, and not merely through personal and interested motives, the firm and fast ally of England. His conduct during the Crimean war proved this to the world. Another anecdote, which I believe has never appeared in print, and which I am able to tell here on the very best authority, will serve to show that he was equally our true ally at the critical period of the Indian mutiny, when, if he had played us false, and allowed himself to be swayed by ambitious motives, the fate and fortune of England itself might have been jeopardized. In the course of a conversation between the Emperor and the late Sir John Bowring at Torquay, in Sept. 1871, the latter remarked that his son, who had been Lord Canning's secretary in India, had gleaned a very valuable collection of autograph letters on Indian subjects. The Emperor remarked that if his own papers had not been burnt in the Tuileries, he could have sup· plied Mr. Bowring with a remarkable document, no less than a letter which he had received at that crisis from the miscreant Nana Sahib, appealing to his Imperial Majesty for aid against the English, who, he asserted, "had invaded all the most cherished privileges of the Hindoo people, and destroyed all their dearest institutions, not allowing them even to burn their own wives!" In fact, that able and indefatigable, poorly rewarded public servant, was always of opinion, from intimate personal acquaintance, that the Emperor was uniformly actuated by the most friendly feelings towards England, even when most bitterly abused and lam· pooned by its press, and he quite ridiculed the idea of any danger of attack on our shores existing in that quarter. It is obvious to remark that for such sincere friendship he ought to be credited with the greater goodness of heart, seeing that it was England who put the crowning stone on the fall of the first Napoleon, by chaining the prisoned eagle on the barren rock of St. Helena.

But to pass from general to particular statements, it may be asked how can it be shown that he was, as I have asserted, the best possible ruler for France as she has been of late years ? I will bring some wit· nesses in proof of my words. "All men," says the *Times,* "can admire genius, courage, and work. All men can, if they will see facts that are plain before their eyes, and acknowledge results by which they themselves have benefited. And that is all that is necessary to enable Englishmen to feel that the Imperial family of France has at this moment a title of no common kind to their good wishes and friendly estimation. That the Emperor, in govern· ing a most impracticable and impulsive people, may not have committed some grave mistakes, is not to be denied ; but who that remembers the France of 1848, and compares it with the France Of the early part of 1870, cannot see the enormous strides in national prosperity which, under the rule of Napo- leon III., the Empire has made? That he had ruled with genius, that he had met emergencies with courage, that he had toiled at the details of administration with unflagging industry, is beyond dispute ; and that through all the complicated affairs of Europe-in the Eastern question, in the Italian question, in the Roman question, in the Danish questiort-he maintained a clear, patent, and avowed policy, England has again and again frankly and fully admitted. While through all-- whatever may have been here thought of his policy in these matters-his loyalty and fidelity to the alliance with England have been at once our boast and our security."

I' In spite of his enemies," says the *Morni, V; Post,* "he has been a great benefactor to France. He has made Revolution, in the real sense of the word, though not an impossible, at least a very difficult achievement. He began by providing a practical solution of the beautiful theory advanced by Louis Blanc, in 1848, of the organization of labour, simply by providing employment for the thousands whom the Executive Government of his time found literally thrown upon their hands. And it is easy to find fault with the manner in which this organization has been effected, and in the lavish expenditure on the capital of France-after all, not out of proportion to the requirements of the time,-and the concentration into the capital of the population, so rapidly increasing, including foreigners, to the tune of 40,000 Germans. He has extended the commerce of the country by encouraging the modern development of trade, and by recognizing the theories which have been so clamorously as·setted for that object. The result is found in the enormous wealth of the country. Witness the recent loan, for which 656 million francs were sub.. scribed in Paris in one day."

"The incidents of the Emperor's life," says the *Saturday Review,* "were so striking, and the indications of his character so unmistakable, that it is easy to seize on the general outlines of his career ; but it is impossible at present to do justice to him artd to his opponents, to balance the bad and good In his life; or to attempt to fix his place in history. There ts one test, however, that may fairly be applied to the memory of a man just dead which is of great value. When his death brings all we know of him rapidly and vividly before our minds, .is it on the good or on the bad we know of him

that we instinctively dwell ? There can be no
hesitation in saying decisively that it is the good
side of the Emperor's life and actions that first
occurs to us ; and that we have to think and remember in order to balance the good with the bad.
His devotedness in friendship, his sublime indiffer-
ence to defeat, his patient preparation for great·
ness, seize on us as we think over his early history, before we allow ourselves to smile at the
recollections of his silly imitations of his uncle and
the absurd eagle of Boulogne. That for twenty
years he kept France quiet, gave her a fair share
of glory, made her rich, contented, and powerful,
and transformed Paris, naturally strikes us as the
main thing ; while the terrors of the *coup d 'ltat,*
the disasters of Mexico, the audacious jobbery of
his satellites, and the ruinous exhaustion of the
finances of Paris, seem subsidiary and compara-
tively unimportant. His generous enthusiasm for
Italy, and what he did for her, outweigh what he
left undone, or what he did to disappoint her ; and
Magenta and Solferino cover the siege of Rome
and his coquetting with the Pope and Mentana,
Above all, this exile dying in England appeals
strongly to the memories and gratitude of Eng ..
lishmen. He was probably at one time the only
man in France who was in heart the friend of Eng·
land. He made the English alliance the basis of
his policy. He repressed the bitterness against
England which at a critical moment threatened to
overflow. He treated Englishmen with friendly

favour and magnificent hospitality. He abolished passports in favour of Englishmen, and while his own subjects had to wait and be examined as if they were convicts, cockneys proudly stepped by uncontrolled, as if they had been beings of a superior race. He borrowed Free Trade from England, and, against the wishes of his people and their representatives, concluded the Treaty of Commerce, not only as a measure financially beneficial to France, but as a means of binding together the two nations by the ties of kindly intercourse."

The *Times* observes that, "with his unquestionable ability and some extraordinary gifts, it must be confessed he owed much to fortune. She repeatedly did wonderful things for him when his circumstances were critical. He came to count with too great confidence on her favours when they were showering down on him, and he drew recklessly on his *prestige* instead of nursing it against gloomier days. It had been his aim to persuade his subjects that he was something more than mortal; when his mishaps proved his mortality, they resented the deception he had practised on them, and trampled their idol in the dust. It is not in our province now to speculate as to the influence of his rule on France, or to examine how far France is to be blamed for the vices and corruption of the Empire. If he misunderstood the people he governed when he treated them rather like children than as men, we can only repeat, the fault was a venial one. Had he been born in a station beneath the influence of those ambitions that tempt men to become criminal, he would have lived distinguished and died esteemed. As it is, if the circle of his devoted friends has sadly dwindled since his fall and abdication, we trust for the honour of human nature that there are many who mourn him sincerely, in common gratitude."

"It is for moralists," says the *Queen*, "to expatiate on the strange fact that both the great Napoleons have died in exile, and both on British soil; the first, it is true, was a captive, and the other as free as Englishmen could make him. Both bowed to the attacks of distressing disease, which must have long preyed upon their vitals. Louis Napoleon has equalled some of the greater glories and deeper woes of his memorable kinsman; but he leaves a name which will be more popular in England, and probably in most parts of Europe. Profound in his calculations, inscrutable in his motives, and mysterious in his action, he was regarded with apprehension by some, who were generally opposed to his policy. He, nevertheless, succeeded in rising to the highest position among the kings and emperors of his time, and his word was powerful enough to dictate war or peace almost whenever he chose. He was a faithful ally to our country during many years, and under all changes. He is a man whose loss will be marked. A great light disappears with him below the world's political horizon. His great ability was shown in so many ways and on so many occasions, that his immense influence cannot be wholly ascribed to the *pres#ge* of his great name and exalted position."

"Least of all," observes the *Echo,* "should England be unkind and censorious towards Louis Napoleon. He had formed many ties with this country. He was naturally fond of Englishmen, and his Court was open to them in particular. He was sedulous and unwearied in his desire to obtain their good opinion. In 1854 he showed much eagerness to obtain our alliance-his enemies accuse him of sacrificing, on that occasion, everything in order to gain it. Throughout the war with Russia he stood by us faithfully. And when times of peace came he showed himself accessible to new ideas coming from England. In youth he had watched the Corn Law agitation, and embraced the principles of Free Trade, and he had the courage to take an Englishman into his councils, and, in concert with Richard Cobden, to force Free Trade upon a somewhat reluctant people. He borrowed from us the idea of industrial exhibitions. His navy imitated ours. He encouraged imitation of our sports. His model farm was copied from English examples. He liked to talk with Englishmen, perhaps, above all foreigners. Those who gained admittance to his court were surprised to find so much that was English in his ways of life. Here he lived the unobtrusive life of an English gentleman. More than once-in particular on the famous roth of April, 1848-the exile of King-street * took upon himself the duties of an English citizen. It was English men and women † who raised money for his *attentat de Boulogne.* It was with Englishmen he ate the famous farewell supper at Crockford's the night before making his unsuccessful *coup* in 1848. At all times he was fond of visiting and patronising what Englishmen delight to see. His very proneness to theatrical -failings led him to try to cultivate, by the rules of contrary, English ways of simplicity. Not a little of the sincere sympathy which to-day is manifested in England springs from the fact that throughout his life he was courteous, and particularly so in regard to Englishmen. All his errors were perpetrated against others, never against us, for the Secret Treaty has never been proved to be directly his work. The invasion panic, which threw this country into convulsions twenty years ago, was due to our own folly, not to his evil designs. He owed England nothing. The disease-worn, care-tortured, lonely man who has just died at Chislehurst was not to the majority of Englishmen "the Man of. Sedan," the ruler whose policy had brought misery and degradation and shame on a

* It may be worthy of a note here, that on the front of the house, No. 2, King Street, has been placed a tablet stating that "Here Louis Napoleon, Emperor of the French, lived, 1838---1840."

† A writer in a contemporary says that the funds which enabled Napoleon to return to France, when he was made First President and then Emperor, were supplied by a Mrs. Howard, who sold an annuity for the purpose of raising the money. For this service she was presented with an estate, and created Countess of Beauregard.

proud nation. We who have not suffered are quick to forget calamities which did not strike us, and in England to-day there will be room for few other thoughts than that he was her unfailing friend, that, true or false to others, he was ever friendly to us. So, with the memory of this in our minds, let no unkind words, for one day at least, be uttered of him whose plots and schemes and sufferings are ended, and whose worldly character passes from the judgment of his perplexed and disputing contemporaries to stand before the bar of History. His life connot be pronounced in a few sentences. The final verdict cannot be huddled up in a few hurried words. For the time we prefer to think of him as one who was stanch in his private friendships, naturally courteous and suave, and felt a real affection for his country."

One single English publication, *Reynold's Newspaper,* enjoys the unenviable distinction of dissenting at this moment from the general expression of English sympathy and appreciation of a man who played a difficult part on the political stage, played for high stakes and lost, had no more faults than any other warlike sovereign of a military people, but who committed the one unpardonable error of not achieving final success! Not only, according to this writer, was the late Emperor a" miserable imbecile both as a general and a statesman," but a " curse to France and a bugbear to Europe," "one of the greatest scoundrels that ever sat upon a throne "-so great indeed that " no bigger scoundrel

ever swung at the Old Bailey." He adds : "Although impotent for further mischief, the world at
large will be thankful that such a dangerous moun-
tebank has been removed from its surface. The
past execrate, the present laughs at and loathes,
and the future will curse and anathematise him as
the scourge of France. And so ends the earthly
career of one whose name, unassociated with scarcely
a single virtue, is linked with more than a thousand
crimes."

It is to be hoped that these words proceed from
the pen of a foreigner, and have been merely translated into English by one who is no more responsible for them than the compositor whose hands
"set them up in type." But be this as it may, it
is certain that they are the deliberate utterances of
Mr. G. M. Reynolds, and were spoken before
the remains of the fallen Emperor had been consigned to the grave. If such is Mr. Reynold's
comment on the saying, *nit nisi bonum de mortuis,*
we may all indeed be glad that there is another
tribunal beyond that of man, where the Emperor's
faults and failings will be more justly weighed.
The English people will refuse to believe, with Mr.
Reynolds, that it was "from the purely selfish
motives of the Bonapartists " that the late war
arose, much less that it was the Emperor or the
Empress-in spite Qf the assertion of M. Thiers-
that goaded and hounded on the French people to
raise the war-cry " *a Berlin."* It was the national
vanity of the French people, intoxicated with the

prosperity and success which their Emperor had given them to drink; and the Bonapartists had no more to do with it, as a party, than the Orleanist or Republican factions.

Certain Continental papers, published in France and elsewhere, affected surprise at the sympathy shown in England to the late Emperor through his illness and at his death ; and one published at Vienna does as much outrage to good taste in its writings as Mr. Reynolds himself. They are astonished that the exile of Chislehurst should receive from us the same consideration as if he had died in his bed of state in the Imperial Tuileries. They show that they know not the English nation, and its real feelings. Here we flatter ourselves that our compassion for misfortune and suffering is not influenced by selfish or political considerations, and that a downfall like that which befell the Emperor at and before Sedan, if it has any effect on our sympathy, tends rather to increase than to diminish it. With the fickle-minded and ungrateful people of Paris it is instinct to turn with the ferocity of a wild beast on a fallen or even unsuccessful leader, or at least to brand him with the stigma of a traitor. They, Christians as they profess to be, like the ass in the fable, rejoice in kicking the dead lion : with Englishmen the words of the heathen philosopher are true, " *res est sacra miser.*"

While, however, to our credit as a people and a nation be it said, such are the kindly and respectful comments of our press upon the life, career, and

character of the discrowned Emperor, who died an
exile on our shores, far different was the reception
of the intelligence at Paris. When Louis Philippe
died at Claremont in 1850, the tongues of Englishmen kept a respectful silence as to his many failings and frailties, and, so far as could be done,
threw a veil over his errors and his sins against
England. So, also, in the body that lay all cold in
the death - chamber at Chislehurst, the English
press almost unanimously recognised a departed
friend, and spoke and wrote of him as warmly as
if he had died the envied wearer of the first crown
in Europe, and the owner of the Tuileries in which
he was born. But the news, we are told, was received at Paris almost without producing any impression. In fact, it was scarcely noticed, even
by the people who sat and lounged about the
Boulevards, and many of whom must have owed
what little fortune they possessed to the prosperity
of the middle-class under the Empire. Consider-
ing the heartless and unchivalrous nature of that
once chivalrous 'and susceptible people, this fact
ought not to cause wonder here, especially when it
is remembered that the news of the death of Napoleon I. at St. Helena fifty years ago produced just
as little of what the newspapers call a " profound
sensation."

Turning next to a view of the late Emperor in
the light of an author, my readers will have already
observed that even before he had attained middle
life, or had aspired to the Presidential Chair, the

Prince had already evidenced the scope and keenness of his intellect by a variety of thoughtful treatises upon many of the most profound, or vital, or practical questions affecting the whole science of government. Besides his " Political Reflections," published in 1832, and his" Historical Fragments," in 1841, as well as his famous work of 1839," The Napoleonic Ideas," and his text-book on "Artillery Past and Present," Prince Louis Napoleon, it was well known, (as I have already said) that he had written vigorously and sagaciously on topics as widely contrasted as Pauperism and the Slave Trade, as the Electoral Laws and the Sugar Question, as the Recruiting System and Military Organization.

Early in the spring of 1862 it was announced that the Emperor was busy on a new work, on a large scale, " The Life of Julius Csesar," It was published in the March of that year; its contents were severely criticised, and he was accused at the time of having composed the work in order to draw out a fictitious parallel between the Founder of the Roman Empire, Julius Csesar, his own uncle, the elder Napoleon, and himself, and to earn for himself a cheap and easy immortality by quietly placing himself on a pedestal side by side with those illustrious and truly great men. What was his real object in issuing such a book, Louis Napoleon may be allowed to explain for himself, in his own words, which I extract from his preface.

"That which precedes sufficiently indicates the

object I have proposed to myself in writing this history. That object is to prove that when Providence raises up such men as Ceesar, Charlemagne, and Napoleon, it is to trace out to nations the path they ought to follow, to stamp a new era with the seal of their genius, and to accomplish in a few years the work of many centuries. Happy the nations who comprehend and follow them ! Woe to those who misunderstand and resist them ! They act like the Jews ; they crucify their Messiah. They are blind and guilty- blind, for they see not the impotence of their efforts to suspend the final triumph of good ; guilty, for they only retard its progress by impeding its prompt and fertile application.

" In fact, neither the assassination of Ceesar nor the imprisonment of St. Helena could destroy beyond revival two popular causes overthrown by a league disguising itself with the mask of liberty. Brutus by killing Cassar plunged Rome into the horrors of civil war ; he did not prevent the reign of Augustus, but he rendered possible those of Nero and Caligula. Nor has the ostracism of Napoleon by conspiring Europe prevented the resuscitation of the Empire, and yet how distant are we from that solution of great questions, from the appeased passions, from the legitimate satisfaction given to nations by the first Empire !

"Thus, ever since 1815 has verified itself that prophecy of the captive of St. Helena:-

" ' What struggles, what bloodshed, what years

will yet be required that the good I wished to do to mankind may be realized ?' In fact, what disturbances, civil wars, and revolutions have occurred in Europe since 1815! In France, in Spain, Italy, Poland, Belgium, Hungary, Greece, and Germany.

"NAPOLEON.

" Palace of the Tuileries,
"March 20, 1862."

The *A thenceum* gives the following estimate o(the Emperor regarded in the light of a political writer:-

" As Napoleon the First made his *dlbttt* in the artillery, and wrote some short strictures on the subject, Prince Napoleon did the same, and while serving as an officer in the Swiss army, gave to the world his 'Manual of Artillery,' a technical work, which was held in some 'esteem in military circles. It may almost be regretted, in a purely literary point of view, that he did not confine himself to a subject for which his disposition for exact sciences suited him ; as the ' Reveries Politiques,' published in Paris in 1833, gave obvious evidence of a limited literary talent, and a persistent desire of identifying himself with Napoleon the First. This was so far perceived in Paris, that the monarchy of July began to watch his career with no small uneasiness. At that time he certainly manifested democratic tendencies, and a glance through Napoleon the First's biography will show an analogy of sentiment altogether striking. The' Reveries Politiques' was followed by a sketch of a constitution, in which the Prince expressed his disbelief in the stability of the State as it had been organized after the Revo-[ution of 1830. His next production followed close on the preceding one : it was a piece of verse, in· scribed to M. de Chateaubriand, in defence of the Duchess de Berry. Whatever opinion may be entertained of the late Emperor's capacities as a writer, all will agree, as all agreed at the time, that his incursion into the field of poetry was by no means a happy one. Strange to say, however, his writings found unexceptional favour with the small nucleus of democrats who were preparing the Revolution of 1848, under the leadership of Armand Carrel.

"Prince Louis Napoleon was next found at work in England, where he sought refuge after his *coup de main* at Strasbourg. He published in London a curious work, in which he undertook to expound and vindicate his uncle's theories. 'Les Idees Napoleoniennes ' deserves special attention. Prince Napoleon has revealed himself in these pages more than he ever did elsewhere. He has assimilated revolutionary ideas with Napoleonism, and made vain efforts to explain that the principles of authority and democracy are not anti· pathetic. How he put his theories in practice has been seen. This curious book had a vast sale in France, and was translated into most European languages.

" His captivity in the Fort of Ham afforded him further leisure to indulge in literature. Here he wrote, almost simultaneously, a dithyrambic poem " to the memory of the great Emperor," and an "Essay on Fulminating Powder." The nature of Prince Napoleon's mind may be judged by the difference of these two productions, the second of which was better written than the first. Among his other prison writings, some Historical Fragments, and an Essay on the " Extinction of Pauperism " may be mentioned. He was equally desirous of trying his hand at journalism, and the tolerance of Louis Philippe enabled him to contribute some political articles to the Democratic papers; but as these articles have been entirely forgotten, we are led to suppose that their value was not remarkable," •

It should be added that the collected edition of the late Emperor's works was published in 1854-57, in four volumes ; but, of course, it does not contain his "Julius Csesar,"

" From the time of his accession to power, the late Emperor was engrossed with public affairs which left him but little time for literary pursuits. The first volume of the ' Life of Csesar ' was issued in 1862, the second in 1866. It has been judged long ago, and the total obscurity into which this work has fallen, and which even the rank of the writer could not prevent, shows what it is worth. "L'Histoire de Jules Cesar' is dry in quality, and its style much resembles that of M.

Duruy, tile boarding-schoolhistorian, who was a Ministerof Public Instruction under the Empire, and whosecontributionsto his master's book are said to have been somewhat extensive. The historical value of the book has been pronounced singularly small; and it is not hazardous to predict that' The Life of Csesar' will not be Napoleon Bonaparte's chief claim to the consideration of posterity; nor do we believe that his literary workswillbe as well remembered as the part he played in history."

Passing lastly to the subject of Louis Napoleon's religion, it is a trite remark that the late Emperor was one of the " best abused" men of his day; but on no ground was he more pertinaciouslyand more senselesslyreviledthan for the .line which he took in support of the Papacy. For the aid which he gave for so many years to "the Papal cause," in other words,to the maintenanceof Pope Pius IX. on his twofold throne, he was constantly reviled at Exeter Hall, by Protestants of unreasoning minds and bigoted views,as a " Jesuit," as " Antichrist," as the "Beast of the Revelations,"as the "Man of Sin." On the other hand, Roman Catholicsof the Ultramontane school taunted him with being a traitor to his Holiness,and a deserter of the cause of religion. Neither of these parties spoke the truth, whichhere, as elsewhere,lay half way between the opposite sides of the matter. He was the "Eldest Son of the Church," not only by title, but also in point of fact, and though in early life, when probably he was not aware of their real intent, he had been a member of the Italian Carbonari, yet, at all events, after his elevation to the Imperial throne and his marriage, he proved himself a loyal son of the Church of which his baptism made him a member, and he never abandoned his recognition of the *spiritual* power of the Papacy, or of St. Peter, and fought for the temporal power of the Roman Pontiff as long as there was a shadow of a shade of fighting for it with success. When his own subjects at Rome declined to live under the feeble secular sway of Pius IX., Louis Napoleon was too wise and far-sighted a politician to allow blood to be shed in a hopeless cause, even if His Holiness would have permitted it ; but pious Roman Catholics who are inclined to blame him for the course which he adopted will do well, in forming their judgments, to remember that he never finally removed his troops from Rome until they were needed for the defence of France after her first reverses in August, 1870, when the last remains of the Pope's temporal power suffered its final collapse.

TIJE END,

www.ingramcontent.com/pod-product-compliance
Lightning Source LLC
Chambersburg PA
CBHW021127020726
47500CB00003B/952